8.99

KU-644-824

GUNSMOKE JUSTICE

Troy Clayton's father had been dry-gulched, so Troy returned to Bender County after seven years away as a gunslinger. He hoped to remain unrecognized, but the mystery men who had framed him with the robbery that had sent him to prison for a year were still in control. Worse still, they had used his absence to pin a murder charge on him. Gradually, Troy began to unravel the mystery but, surrounded by hot lead, nothing could prepare him for the shocking surprise that lay in store.

CORBA SUNMAN

GUNSMOKE JUSTICE

Complete and Unabridged

LINFORD
Leicester

First published in Great Britain in 2001 by
Robert Hale Limited
London

First Linford Edition
published 2002
by arrangement with
Robert Hale Limited
London

British Library CIP Data

Sunman, Corba
    Gunsmoke justice.—Large print ed.—
Linford western library
    1. Western stories
    2. Large type books
    I. Title
    823.9'14 [F]

    ISBN 0–7089–9950–6

Published by
F. A. Thorpe (Publishing)
Anstey, Leicestershire

Set by Words & Graphics Ltd.
Anstey, Leicestershire
Printed and bound in Great Britain by
T. J. International Ltd., Padstow, Cornwall

This book is printed on acid-free paper

1

The sun was swinging low behind the distant mountains when Troy Clayton reached home range after an absence of seven years. But he had no eyes for the rugged scenery that was burned in his memory, and none of the rage and hatred remained that had tarnished his mind during the early days of his flight from all that he had loved. His memory was filled with scars that would never fade, but he had covered them over with a layer of violent deeds on the turbulent trail that had led him into the great south-west of the country; through Texas, New Mexico and Arizona.

He had left his mark in the form of a dozen graves across the bleak, unforgiving land he had traversed, hiring out his gun to make a stand against bad men of the type he had left in control here in

Bender County. But always in the back of his mind had been the knowledge that one day he would have to return to face the rotten set-up that had chased him out with his tail between his legs.

He had not expected to return under the circumstances awaiting him. Word had reached him via the back trails that his father had been shot in the back and lay on the point of death. Despite the bad blood between them, it was Clayton blood, and he was back to take on the grim chore he should never have run from in the first place. But he had been just a raw kid in those days. Now he was a different proposition.

For all he knew his father might now be dead and buried. He had been riding eastward for three weeks, keeping to unfrequented trails and avoiding those areas where law reigned and unknown enemies lurked.

He was a big man, over six feet tall, wide shouldered and powerfully built. He was lean, aged twenty-four, with deep-set blue eyes, fair hair that curled from under his black Stetson, and with an assumed expression that was habitually hard, the flat planes of his face taut and set in grim lines. He was dressed in range garb; faded blue denims and a leather vest, with a black neckerchief lying in dusty folds at his throat. A large Colt .45 pistol rode low on his right hip, the well-oiled holster tied down to facilitate a fast draw. The butt of a Winchester protruded from a saddle scabbard under his right leg.

He had planned to arrive in Sunset Ridge after dark, and welcomed the long blue shadows creeping across the range. The sun finally departed and night swooped in, dense and impenetrable, but he knew this range well enough to cross it blindfold, and rode steadily, finding the going easier when the stars and the moon brightened to bathe the plains with an ethereal glow. He would not go directly to the Tented C ranch because he was not aware of the situation there. Instead, he was making for the town, and a thread of animation unwound in his mind when he thought of Helen Vail, the girl he had planned to marry before being run off the range by the crookedness and greed of unknown men. But he cut off the strand of emotion before it could take hold. He didn't want to think of the old days.

It was an hour after sundown when he reached the western outskirts of Sunset Ridge. Reining in, he sat motionless on his big black gelding, studying the lights of the adobe structures lining the main street. It was a sight he had never thought to see again, and his grim features hardened into even deeper lines as he fought down the bad memories of the past. The knowledge that this peaceful scene had existed every day while he had been forced to be in other parts of the country hurt like a kick in the guts, and he urged the horse into motion, consoling himself with the knowledge that his day would come. Someone would pay for the troubles that had befallen him — the least of which had been one year's hard labour in the state prison.

He entered the town. His hatbrim was pulled low over his blue eyes, and he watched the shadows alertly, wondering if, after an absence of seven years, he could be recognized by sight alone. He doubted it. Since leaving he had changed from a raw youth into a hard-bitten man toughened by the rigours of his environment and the tough life he had led.

He was recalling the past now; all the times he had happily ridden into Sunset Ridge, unaware that all too soon he would be cut off from everything he loved. The shame of his younger son being found guilty of robbery had caused his father to turn his back upon him, and, before he was hauled off to prison to serve his sentence, he had been warned by his older brother, Howard, never to return. As far as the Clayton family were concerned, he was already dead and buried, shamed beyond redemption and no longer acknowledged as a member of the family.

He dropped a hand to the butt of his pistol. There was a man around town he wanted to face before he moved on, whatever the condition of his father. Pete Bolam's lying evidence had sent him to prison. At the time there had been nothing Clayton could do about the injustice, but now he was back in the county he would take it up where it had been dropped.

A shadowy figure stepped off the sidewalk on the right and moved into the centre of the wide street as if to intercept him. Clayton tensed, instinctively. He knew he was asking for trouble riding in openly, but figured no one knew he was coming so there shouldn't be a reception committee. The figure halted in the middle of the street and waited. Clayton reined in when the gelding's muzzle touched the man's shoulder. Street lamps were few and far between, but the beams of the

6

nearest threw glints upon the badge pinned to the man's chest.

'Just a moment, friend. I'm checking out everyone in town tonight. Get off that hoss and let me take a good look at you. I figure you're a stranger.'

'You figure right.' Clayton stepped down from the saddle and trailed his reins, keeping his right hand well away from his gun. 'I reckon on staying the night and riding on in the morning.'

'What's your name? Where are you from, and where are you going?'

'I answer to the handle of Buck Ritson.' Clayton used his mother's maiden name. 'I'm from Idaho, and I'm heading back there soon as I've settled some local business.'

'Uhuh! What business would that be?'

'Are you looking for someone in particular? If so you can see I'm not him. There couldn't be another around like me.'

'I don't know 'bout that. The feller I'm watching for is six foot two, big as a barn, and hell on wheels with a gun. He's buried more than a dozen men in the last seven years. You're the same size, friend, even if your name ain't Troy Clayton. I'm gonna take you in so Sheriff Kline can give you the onceover. He knows Clayton by sight. It'd be more than my job is worth to let you go by.'

'You ain't taking me anywhere,' Clayton was alerted by the mention of the sheriff's name. Hondo Kline had been top lawman in Bender County for twenty years, and was the last man Clayton wanted to see. 'I ain't breaking any law and I'm tired and hungry. I'm gonna take care of my hoss and then look out for myself. You wanta check on me then do it after I've handled my chores.'

'The hell you say!' The deputy dropped his right hand to the butt of his holstered gun. 'You'll do like I say, pilgrim, or it'll go hard with you.'

Clayton reached out with his left hand and grasped the deputy's wrist as the man pulled his gun. The weapon exploded raucously but the muzzle was pointing skyward and the slug whined harmlessly into the night. Clayton slid his right foot forward a pace, transferred his weight to it, then unleashed a right-hand punch that battered the man's jaw. The deputy's head rocked back and he dropped instantly, out cold, his gun spilling from his hand.

The echoes of the shot faded quickly and Clayton looked around, his eyes narrowed. A man appeared out of the shadows nearby and came at a run toward him.

'Hey, Slick, have you got him?' he called. 'Is it Clayton?'

Clayton remained motionless, facing the man. The newcomer drew nearer, then paused.

'You ain't Slick!' he gasped, reaching for his gun.

Clayton drew his gun and thumbed back the hammer in one fast, flowing motion. The other man was fast, clearing leather almost as quickly, but

Clayton's gun blasted first and the newcomer spun around and fell on his face, his gun putting a slug into the dust almost between his feet. Echoes chased away across the town.

Clayton grimaced as he looked around. He grasped his reins, led the horse around the motionless figures, and moved off to the left, seeking an alley he knew was there although he could not see it. The darkness was impenetrable, especially in the gaps between the street lamps. He found the alley and moved into it, and had to feel his way along with his left hand touching the building on that side.

As he reached the far end of the alley a gunshot exploded back on the street, and the deputy he had stunned began raising an alarm in a raucous voice. Clayton shook his head, cursing his bad luck, and went on to the back lots. A square of yellow lamplight marked the presence of a cabin, and Clayton made for it, moving warily.

'What was that shooting?' A low voice

spoke from the dense shadows by the lighted window as Clayton approached. 'Stand still. I got a gun on you.'

'Barney. I recognize your voice. I figured you'd still be living here.'

'Who in hell is that?' came the startled reply.

'Troy Clayton. I got word my father was shot so here I am! Right now I need to get my horse under cover.'

'Jeez! You took a risk riding into town, Troy. Put your hoss in the lean-to and I'll let you in the back door. Be quick. There ain't nowhere safe in town for you.'

Clayton smiled cynically as he went around to the back, feeling his way along the side wall of the cabin. That was an understatement if ever he'd heard one. He was not safe anywhere in the entire United States! He found the lean-to and led the gelding into it. The back door of the cabin opened and a glimmer of light shone from the covered lamp held by the short, round-shouldered man who emerged.

'Troy. I'm glad to see you! It's been a long time.'

'Is Dad still alive?'

'Sure is. He ain't out of the wood yet but the doc reckons he'll pull through. It's been touch and go, Son. But Henry Clayton is one tough *hombre* and it'd take more than one bullet to put him in his box.'

Clayton heaved a silent sigh of relief as he stripped the gear from his horse. Draper set the lamp on a convenient box and turned up the wick. He was short in build, running to fat, pushing sixty now, and he moved stiffly, his joints complaining of the many years he had spent in the saddle in all kinds of weather. He grinned as he looked at Clayton, and nodded.

'You've sure filled out some, Troy. It's good to see you, Son. I been hearing all about your doings on the trail, and never expected to see you again in this life. But when your pa was shot I knew you'd come back, although it's a bad move on your part. The sidewinders running this county are expecting you. In fact I figure your pa was shot just to bring you back so they could nail you permanent. They've always been scared you'd return, and likely they're planning even bigger things these days. There's been nothing but talk about your return for the last coupla weeks. Have you been out to Tented C yet?'

'No. I figured to drop in on Helen to pick up all the news, but got stopped on the street by a deputy.'

'Helen's out at Tented C, nursing your pa. I heard the shooting just now. Did you kill the deputy?'

'Nope. I put him out cold. But there was a second man I had to shoot. He could be dead.'

'You must have tangled with Slick Porter, the chief deputy. He figures he's the big gun around here now Hondo Kline ain't so active. Porter ain't been in the county more than a year so you won't know him. But you remember Kline, huh, Troy?'

'I ain't never forgotten him. It'll be a

pleasure to see him again, but not tonight. But Pete Bolam is a horse of another colour. Is he still around?'

Draper pulled a pail of water forward so Clayton's horse could drink. He grunted as he straightened, and then fetched a forkful of hay from a heap in a corner and pitched it into a narrow trough. His eyes were slitted, had almost disappeared in his fleshy face, and he looked at Clayton for a moment without speaking. Then he shook his head.

'Bolam headed north a coupla weeks ago, soon as there was talk about you coming back. I figure it was Bolam shot your pa, Troy, figuring it would bring you back. But I reckon he ain't keen to face you.'

'I'll face him before I'm through.' Clayton's eyes were narrowed and bleak. 'What's Howard doing these days?'

'You know your brother better than most, I reckon.' Draper shrugged. 'I ain't had nothin' to do with him since they carted you away. I know things ain't never been right between you two, Son, and they could get even worse now.'

'Why's that?'

Draper shuffled his feet and then turned to get a dipper of oats from a barrel, which he put in the trough for the horse. He looked at Clayton, still shaking his head.

'I reckon you're gonna get the word before long so it won't matter if I put you straight now. Howard is fixing to marry Helen.'

Clayton's lips pulled tight as he considered. 'Has she consented to marry him?'

'I can't answer that.'

Clayton heaved a sigh. 'Yeah, well, I guess it ain't any of my business,' he decided. 'I've been away too long for any of it to matter. As I recall, there never was an understanding between Helen and me, so she can marry who she wants. I ain't had any contact with her since the day I went to prison.'

'And there wasn't any way you could come back without running your neck into a noose.' Draper shook his head. 'Just after you were released from prison someone robbed and killed old Frank Butler. Remember him? He had the saddlery on Main Street. You were blamed for that, Troy, and Kline even went to the trouble of putting out dodgers for you, with a reward of five hundred dollars offered, dead or alive.'

Clayton digested the information in silence, a muscle working in his cheek as he clenched his teeth. He straightened his shoulders and placed his saddle on a rail.

'I didn't know about that,' he admitted. 'They sure meant for me to stay away, huh?'

'I never believed you did it, Troy. Like you say, they was making sure you couldn't come back. But come on in and I'll get supper for you. I figure you must have been on the trail for weeks.'

'Ever since I heard about Pa. Nearly three weeks, far as I can judge. You reckon I'll be safe here?' Clayton shook his head even as he asked the question. 'Barney, I reckon Kline will think of you soon as he hears I've showed up in town.'

'Yeah. You could be right.' The oldster grinned, showing tobacco-stained teeth. 'Listen, Troy, if there's any way I can help you in this then speak up. You got that? I've been itching to take a hand in this game ever since they hauled you off to prison but I've held off because I'm too old to handle it alone. But I'll side you now, Son. Just gimme the word. I've been praying you would return. I wrote you after you contacted me when you left jail but you never wrote again, and I didn't even know if you got my letter. In it I told you I'd quit cold at Tented C. Couldn't stand the place with you gone in disgrace. And Howard never made it easy for me.'

'Don't get mixed up in it, Barney. I plan to put the record straight and settle a few old scores. At the time it happened I didn't have an idea who or what was back of it, but over the years I've had plenty of time to think about it. I reckon Hudson Brady started it but I don't know why. I have heard he's taken over most of the town while I've been gone. But what I don't understand is why he figured I was a danger to him; a raw kid still wet behind the ears. That's what I could never figure out — why he wanted me outa the way.'

'I reckon you're right about Brady. But he allus covered his tracks all ways to the middle, and with the law in his pocket there ain't no way you can pin anything on him. He's got enough men around him to do his dirty work with no questions asked. You're gonna have to play your cards close to your vest, Troy. When word gets out you're back all hell is gonna bust loose. Mebbe you should turn right around and ride back to where you came from. They're playing for high stakes, Son, and you'll get trampled for sure if you try to make a stand against them.'

'I'll take my chances.' Clayton dropped a hand to his holstered gun and caressed the smooth butt. 'There are some men that I wanta see through gunsmoke, Barney, and I won't even think of leaving before I've done that. They had their fun with me, and took seven years outa my life. Now it's my turn, and I'm sure gonna make them pay.'

'Always watch your back, Son.'

Clayton nodded. 'Can I leave my horse here? I don't wanta drop you into any trouble, but I need to scout around town and pick up the threads again. I need to do it before folks realize I'm back in the county.'

'Sure. I'll take care of the nag. But be careful, Troy.'

Clayton nodded and took his leave, his thoughts busy on the information he had gleaned. He hadn't thought it would be easy to come back, and there was a charge of murder against him that he had not known about. His anger flared but he fought it down. It wouldn't do to go off half-cocked. He had to fight these men with the same kind of cunning and forethought they had used to frame him in the first place.

He went silently through the darkness to the main street, and stood in the mouth of the alley to look around. A number of figures were on the sidewalk outside the law office, and he heard excited voices discussing the attack on the two men. A breeze was blowing along the street and its intensity made his eyes water. He considered his options, and realized he could do nothing around here. He needed to go out to the ranch and see his father. Perhaps he could get his brother Howard to back him, although there had never been any love lost between them because Howard had always made it plain that, for some unknown reason, he disliked his younger brother.

Hunger pangs gnawed at his insides and he went along the street looking for an eating-house, keeping in the dense shadows. Supper would be almost over now, and he needed to eat in order to be ready to fight or run. If they discovered his whereabouts and started pursuing him it might be a long time before his next meal.

He passed several men on the sidewalk, but the darkness concealed his features and no one raised an alarm. His confidence grew as he paused at the batwings of a saloon and peered into the lighted interior. He nodded slowly when he recognized some of the faces inside. It seemed that nothing had changed around here during his absence. Life was going on normally for everyone but himself.

The men in front of the law office suddenly moved away to hurry off in different directions. Clayton guessed they were about to search the town for him. He eased the gun in his holster and mentally alerted himself for trouble. He had no intention of getting caught, and was ready to kill to stay out of jail.

He found an eating-house but it was

closed. The door was locked. Inside, a waitress was putting chairs upon the small tables and a man was swabbing the floor with a mop and bucket.

Clayton turned away and found a man standing just behind him, wearing a law star on his shirt and twin guns around his waist. He looked like the deputy who had stopped him earlier, and Clayton instantly swung his right fist, crashing his hard knuckles against the man's jaw. The deputy uttered a cry of surprise and went over backwards. His heels caught on something and he crashed heavily on the sidewalk.

Clayton moved away quickly, losing himself in the shadows. He found an alley and went along it to the back lots, telling himself that this was no good. They had been expecting his arrival and were prepared to take him. He needed to get clear and rethink his intentions before it was too late.

Crossing the back lots, he returned to Barney Draper's cabin, and dropped a hand to his gun when he saw the door was open. Barney was in the doorway, talking to two men, and as Clayton moved in silently one of the callers pushed the old man back inside the cabin and entered swiftly, a gun gripped in an upraised hand.

Clayton went forward quickly, lifting his gun from its holster. He was close on the heels of the second man as he went in through the doorway, and was in time to see the first man crash the barrel of his gun against Barney's skull. The oldster went down like a bale of hay and lay crumpled on the floor, blood spurting from a gash opened up on his forehead.

'When I ask a question I expect a straight answer!' the man cursed, standing over the unconscious oldster. He kicked Barney in the ribs. 'Come on. Get up. You ain't hurt. We know you're a friend of Troy Clayton.'

'Someone mentioned my name,' Clayton rasped.

The man nearest him swung around quickly, his right hand grabbing at the butt of his holstered gun. Clayton back-handed him across the face, using the barrel of his sixgun. The man uttered a cry of pain and went sprawling backward, falling against a table before crashing to the floor. The man who had hit Barney spun around, lifting his gun, and Clayton had no option but to shoot. He triggered his gun, aiming for the man's right shoulder. The cabin was rocked by the thunderclap explosion and Clayton's ears protested at the noise. The man staggered backward, his gun spilling from his hand. A splotch of blood appeared on the front of his shirt as he hit the floor on his back and relaxed.

Clayton clenched his teeth, furious with the way the situation was turning against him. He had hoped to go about his business silently and without hindrance. He checked both men, then turned his attention to Barney, who was beginning to stir.

'How you feeling, Barney? Are you

hurt bad?' Clayton was concerned for the old man.

'Gimme a coupla minutes and I'll be all right.' Draper fingered the swelling growing on his head. 'I guess a little knock ain't gonna hurt me none.'

Clayton helped the oldster to his feet, pulling forward a chair and seating him, then having to hold him upright until Barney was sufficiently recovered from the blow.

'Who are these two men?' he demanded. 'They're not wearing law badges.'

Barney shook his head. 'I've seen 'em around town recently but I sure as hell don't know who they work for. They been spending most of their time in the saloons, drinking and playing poker. Looks like they've been waiting for you to show up, Troy. They asked for you when I opened the door to them. I guess they got me pegged as a friend of yours.'

'I'm gonna have to make tracks, and fast.' Clayton's eyes were hooded, filled with conjecture. 'They're ready for me around here, and I ain't keen to get put out of this a second time. You better ride with me, Barney. If I leave you here these two will work on you some more. You'll have to make yourself scarce for a time. Do you feel up to riding?'

'Yeah. And I guess you're right.' Barney staggered when he moved. 'We better up stakes, Troy, and get the hell out. I got a bronc in the livery barn along the street. You better fix these two so they can't take after us. Have you killed that skunk who hit me?'

'I reckon he'll live.' Clayton looked at the wounded man. The bullet hole was high in the right shoulder. 'I guess he won't be hitting anyone for some time to come.' He turned his attention to the second man, who was groaning and stirring, his features bloodied and swollen from contact with Clayton's gun. 'Grab anything you want to take with you, Barney. I'll saddle up and we'll split the breeze. I guess I have to play my hand a whole lot smarter than this to have any chance of beating this set-up.'

'Now you're talking.' Barney forced a grin. 'Let's get outa here and fight this bunch the way it should be done. You're smart enough to swing the deal, and I'm gonna back you all the way.'

Clayton saddled up, filled with misgiving at having involved Barney. He didn't want to be responsible for anyone else. But the situation had turned against him and he needed to get clear. By the time he was ready to travel, Barney had filled a gunny sack with supplies.

They crossed the back lots to the stable and, when Barney had collected his horse, they rode off into the darkness. Clayton headed towards the distant Tented C ranch. He was going to see his father, and no one, but no one, would stop him.

2

They rode at a comfortable jog through the night, silent for the most part, each knowing the range intimately. Clayton was introspective, his thoughts worrying at the situation like a dog with an old bone, his mind filled with imponderable questions. He was surprised that the whole town expected his arrival. That meant someone was afraid of him. He smiled grimly, for he meant to see that justice came to this county even if he had to use his gun to accomplish it.

A tide of sadness engulfed him as they continued. His homecoming had not been what he hoped for. Innocent in the first place, he had paid a debt to society which others considered he owed, but that had not been the end of it. After his release from prison he had been framed for a murder, and now he was embroiled in a war, not to prove his innocence but to save his life. And the trouble that had befallen him had also been visited upon his father. The old man had been shot in the back for no good reason.

Barney's voice dragged him from his thoughts. The old man's tone was urgent.

'Riders coming up from behind, Troy. I reckon we better get to cover.'

Clayton glanced over his shoulder but could see nothing in the shadows. But the sound of approaching hoofs was loud and rapidly getting louder. An urgency filled him.

'To the left, Barney.' He pointed to a large clump of brush and they turned their horses off the trail and rode into the denser darkness of deep cover. Moments later two riders passed them, riding hell for leather at a pace that was reckless in the night.

'Heck, they're sure splitting the breeze,' Barney observed. 'Do you reckon the town is on fire?'

'Something has sparked them off,

and I don't have to think hard to find a reason. They're in an all-fired hurry to tell someone that Troy Clayton is back in the county.'

'Yeah. That's what I reckon. You know the best thing you can do, Troy?'

'Tell me.'

'Turn your hoss around and ride outa here. You ain't gonna be able to help your pa, and you'll only get yourself killed if you stay on. The set-up is too big for you to handle. Ride away from this. Lose yourself in another State and get on with your life. I'm about the only man in this here county who believes you're innocent, and I sure as hell don't know why you've been picked on. So get out while you can. You can't do any good around here.'

'I guess you're right, Barney, and I agree with what you say. But I'm a Clayton, and family blood has been spilled. I couldn't ride out now even if I wanted to. I'm caught up in this and I ain't running from what I see as my duty. I'll stick with it even if it kills me. I couldn't run and live with myself afterwards.'

'You allus was a hard-head!' Barney chuckled harshly. 'I guess you're hooked in this, and I ain't got no room to talk because the minute you showed up I threw in my hand with you. So we better get smart. You can't ride into Tented C like you own it. You ain't gonna be welcome anywhere in this county, so don't go running your neck into a noose. I taught you how to play poker, among other things, and the rules of that game apply to this business.'

'I need to see my father and find out how he is. Then I want to find out why he was shot and who did it.'

'They'll be ready for you at the ranch. You can't ride in there like you'd be welcome, Troy.'

'What are you trying to tell me? That I'd be taken by my own family and handed over to the law?'

'I ain't trying to say anything, just

31

warning you to watch your step. Those two riders who passed us. Where'd you reckon they're heading?'

'Tented C, I guess.' Clayton frowned. 'They wouldn't be riding to warn my pa, that's for sure. So it's gotta be Howard. Well I don't expect Howie to put out any welcome signs for me. We never did see eye to eye. But I can't believe he's an enemy.'

'Just watch your step,' Barney insisted. 'That way you won't walk into something you can't handle. Howard was always a difficult cuss, but he's changed some while you've been away, Troy. He didn't like the way you dragged the family name into the dust. He acts like a man who can't hold up his head because of what he figures you did.'

'Let's get on,' Clayton said curtly, and they resumed the trail in silence.

Dawn was clawing at the overhead darkness with grey fingers when they finally reined up and sat their weary horses on a low ridge to look down across a wide valley. The glint of a meandering stream showed here and there in the gloom to mark its sparkling surface of water, pointing out its tortuous course as it twisted sharply to nudge its rippling way past a clustered group of buildings.

The tip of the sun showed above the eastern horizon, and, by its growing light, Clayton picked out details of the ranch where he was born. He stared in silence at the familiar scene, and a sense of remoteness filled him as he considered the many times in the past years when he had dreamed of returning to this very spot. Now he was here and there was no joy in him.

'You ain't planning to ride in there, are you?' Barney demanded.

'Not with you siding me. But I can get in there alone before the place wakes up and take a look around. I need to learn things before I can work out how to fight this set-up, Barney, and I don't wanta run you into trouble. You've already done too much to help me. Those men who came to your cabin ain't gonna forget that I turned up and helped you. Stay here until I get back, huh?'

'The hell you say! I ain't letting you outa my sight for a minute, Son. You need a calming influence on you, and that's where I come in.'

'Whoever is out to get me is ready to shoot on sight. That was proved back in town. So you better keep your distance from me, Barney. Lead poisoning is mighty contagious. Stay up here in cover and I'll sneak down into the ranch, find out what I wanta know, and get back before you miss me.'

'I know I can't make you change your mind once it's made up.' Barney shook his head. 'But I don't like it, Troy. If you run into trouble down there I'm like to get myself killed trying to pull you out of it.'

'If I get involved in anything like that then you light out fast and keep going, because I'll be too far gone to need help.'

They turned back from the ridge and sought cover. Clayton left Barney with the horses. The older man's face was plain in the growing daylight, and he looked uneasy as Clayton checked his gun and prepared to move out.

'It's a hard thing for a man to learn, Troy, but there ain't no one down there you can turn to, Son. Don't forget that. Trust no one. Not even Helen.'

Clayton nodded and moved back to the ridge. He paused to look around, then went forward resolutely, staying in cover as he walked down the long slope towards the buildings a quarter mile away. There was no movement around the ranch. Daylight was beginning to filter into the valley, chasing out even the most reluctant shadows, and only the gurgling of the swift moving stream broke the heavy silence of dawn.

Keeping to cover where he could, and crawling where there was no cover, Clayton worked his way in close to the bunkhouse on the left of the big yard and sited fifty yards from the barn. The ranch house was a hundred yards to the right of the barn and very close to the stream. A number of smaller buildings were dotted around the clearing in which the ranch headquarters stood, and there were two corrals to the rear of the barn; one containing a number of horses. The big two-storey ranch house was far to the right and quite apart from all other buildings.

There was noise coming from the bunkhouse, and as Clayton reached the rear corner of the long building the door was opened and six cow-boys emerged to hurry over to the cook shack, talking vociferously. He remained in cover and watched them, aware of his own hunger. He moved around the bunkhouse and headed for the barn, determined to get to the ranch house. He figured that his only chance of success was to contact Helen and risk her displeasure. He did not think she would raise an alarm, whatever her personal feelings about him.

By now the sun was high enough in the sky to throw its light directly into the valley. Shadows had disappeared and there was no cover anywhere. Clayton shook his head, wishing he had arrived an hour earlier. He remained in the shelter of the barn and checked out the area, his blue eyes narrowing when he spotted two men sitting on rocking chairs positioned on the front porch of the house. Sunlight glinted on a law badge one of the men was wearing.

These were the two men who had passed him on the trail. It looked as if Sheriff Kline was taking no chances. But it was obvious to anyone with half a brain that if Troy Clayton rode into the county the first place he would visit was the Tented C.

A man emerged from the cook shack and came striding purposefully toward the barn. At first Clayton thought he had been spotted, but the man made for the big barn door and dragged it open. He disappeared inside for several minutes, then emerged and went off toward the corrals. A second man emerged from the shack and strode toward the ranch house.

Clayton watched the ranch slowly coming to life, impatient to get moving himself. But with two lawmen on the porch he had to play it safe.

He saw a tall figure emerge from the house and stand on the porch to look around. Apparently satisfied with what he saw, he turned to chat to the two lawmen. A pang stabbed through Clayton when he recognized his brother Howard, who was three years his senior. He could not help wondering why Howard had never liked him. There had been bad blood between them for as long as Troy could remember.

A woman emerged from the house and Clayton caught his breath when he recognized Helen Vail. He had been in love with her before his troubles started, but during the ensuing years, he had got used to the idea that she was not for him. Now he looked at her as if they were strangers, but emotion was vibrant in his breast and he had to fight against the anger that welled up inside him.

Howard spoke briefly to the girl, then left the porch and walked across to the corrals. The man who had visited the barn was already saddling a horse, and, when the animal was ready for the trail, Howard took the reins, stepped up into the saddle and rode off in the direction of Sunset Ridge.

Clayton clenched his hands as he watched his brother canter out of sight. Howard had gotten away with everything. No one had framed him for a robbery, and he had spent the last seven years right here at home.

Helen re-entered the house and one of the two lawmen got up and followed her. Clayton moved around the back of the barn and started walking away from the ranch, keeping the barn between himself and any prying eyes. He reached a gully fifty yards back and dropped into it, then followed it until he was level with the rear of the house. He had not used this particular route since he was a boy, when he needed to get around the ranch unseen by his brother Howard.

When he reached the rear of the house he moved up to the lip of the gully and peered around, to find himself gazing at Howard, who was sitting his horse and looking like he expected his younger brother to appear at that very spot.

'So it is you!' Howard leaned forward in the saddle, his face set in grim lines. 'I thought I saw you skulking by the barn. I know your ways, Troy. You've got a helluva nerve coming here with half the lawmen in the county watching for you. What do you want?'

'Ain't that obvious? I heard Pa was shot in the back and I need to know how he is.'

'He won't want to see you. Show your face around him and he'll most likely send for Kline.'

'How is Pa?' Troy climbed out of the

gully and stood at the head of Howard's horse, looking up at his brother with defiance in his pale eyes.

Howard Clayton was tall, lean and wiry, but looked older than his thirty years. It seemed as if all the sap had been burned out of his flesh by the sun and the ravages of the harsh land in which he lived. His eyes were a faded blue, set deep and narrow, and they regarded Troy with an intensity which the younger man found slightly disconcerting. He was dressed in a black broadcloth suit, and, despite the heat, had a bow tie fastened tightly at his throat. A broad leather cartridge-belt was buckled around his lean waist, from the holster of which protruded the handle of a Remington .44 pistol. The holster was not tied down, but Troy knew his brother was fast on the draw.

'Henry is doing all right now.' Howard spoke as if the words burned his thin lips. 'But I figure seeing you would set him back some weeks. You made a mistake coming here. The law was expecting you to make that move and they're ready for you. Kline is no fool. He's been on the look-out for your return ever since you got out of prison. If you have any sense at all you'll go back to where you came from. There's no one around here wants to see you.'

Troy responded with a smile, but there was a cutting pain in his chest. He was worse than a stranger here. He looked up at his brother, shaking his head obstinately.

'I've come a long ways to see Pa and I sure as hell mean to. I wanta know what happened; who shot him and why. Was he robbed?'

'We don't know what happened. Pa ain't conscious. Something to do with the bullet clipping a nerve, or something, so the doctor says.'

'And you say he's doing all right? What kind of all right is that? Have you tried to find who shot him?'

'The law is doing all it can. I know Kline. He's a good man, despite what you think of him.'

'That's your opinion. I got a different view of the local law. Kline couldn't find his mouth unless it was open. He let me go to prison for a robbery I didn't do, and saddled me with a murder when I came out. Someone around here sure as hell wanted me outa the way, huh?'

'You don't have to lie to me, Troy.' Howard shook his head. 'I'm your brother, remember? I've known you from the day you was born. You've always had a wild streak in you, and when you didn't get your own way you struck out, no matter who was in your way. You've brought disgrace to the Clayton name and there's no way back for you. Now you better leave. I'm on my way to town, and when I get there I'll inform Kline of your presence here. That'll give you five hours at least to get clear of the county, so don't stick around. Light out, keep going, and don't ever come back. That's good advice, Troy.'

Howard wheeled his horse and set off

at a canter. Troy gazed after him. When his brother disappeared from sight he stood looking at the ground, lost in thought as he digested Howard's harsh words. But he had no intention of following his brother's advice. Jerking himself free of the hurtful thoughts running through his mind, he strode to the rear of the house, loosening his gun in its holster. He didn't care who came to stop him. He was going to do what he figured he had to.

He had no doubt that Howard would make good his threat. His brother would inform Sheriff Kline of their meeting the minute he reached Sunset Ridge. So that gave him some hours in which to handle the business that had brought him here, and he would let nothing sway him from his course of action.

He gained the rear of the house. The kitchen door was unlocked and he entered silently, stopping short on the threshold when he saw Helen inside. She was making coffee, intent on what she was doing, and not immediately aware of his presence.

He looked at her with the eyes of a stranger, seeing her for the first time in seven years. Her oval face, framed with chestnut curls, he still found good to look upon. There was strength in her attractive features, and he remembered how she had a strict sense of right and wrong. She was wearing a plain grey dress which did not conceal the lines of her figure, and Clayton felt the charm of her tugging at his senses, informing him that the attraction she had always held for him was still there, albeit buried beneath the bitter layers of his harsh living.

'Helen.' His voice almost broke on the word and he clenched his teeth as unaccustomed emotion filled him.

She was startled, and turned her head quickly to look at him. He heard her sharp intake of breath, and a shadow crossed her smooth features.

'Troy!' Helen's voice, pitched low, contained no surprise. 'I've been wondering when you would show up.' There was a coolness in her tone which made her sound prim. 'You'd better be careful. There are two deputies sitting on the porch, hoping to set eyes on you. The whole county is expecting you to come here, and they're ready for you.'

'I know.' He nodded. 'How is my father?'

'As well as can be expected.' She shook her head, signifying despair although her tone was filled with hope. 'It's a bad business, Troy. Henry deserved better than this. He's suffered greatly over the last seven years.'

'I want to see him.'

She nodded when he had been expecting a refusal. 'He's unconscious but you can see him. You've only just missed seeing Howard. He rode out a few minutes ago.'

'I didn't miss him.' Clayton's blue eyes narrowed. 'He's gonna report my presence to Kline soon as he reaches town.'

'Then you must get away!' Fear

showed in her dark eyes.

'I've got plenty of time.' He shrugged, indifferent to his fate. 'I'd like some of that coffee you're making, and I'd sure appreciate anything you've got in the way of food. I ain't eaten in twenty-four hours. It was hectic in town last night and I was unable to get some food.'

'You've been in town? But they're waiting for you to show up there.'

'I discovered that pretty quick. They were keen to gun me down, also anyone who looked like being on my side.'

'You've made a bad name for yourself over the years you've been away.' There was no emotion in her tone but her eyes were filled with sadness. She turned and busied herself preparing a meal for him.

'I never did a thing I was ashamed of,' Troy responded, using the words as a challenge. 'You shouldn't believe everything you heard about me.'

She glanced at him, her eyes filled

47

with a cool expression, and he clenched his hands.

'Sure, I've killed men!' he rapped. 'I hired out my gun to those who needed to fight bad men. But I never murdered anyone. They all had a fair chance to beat me.'

'That wasn't much of a chance, knowing your speed with a gun. But I wasn't referring to your exploits after you left this range. What sticks in my craw is the violent robbery that put you away, and the murder you committed after you got out of prison.'

'What chance do I have of proving my innocence if even you believe I'm guilty? I thought you knew me better, Helen. I told the truth at my trial. Pete Bolam said he saw me commit the robbery but he was lying. Just why he did that I mean to find out. As for the murder, I didn't know a thing about it until Barney Draper told me when I saw him last night.'

'I wish I could believe that.' She put a big pan on the stove and prepared to cook breakfast for him. Troy sat down at a corner of the table, watching her movements, filled with bitterness. He was doomed to shun any kind of a normal life and ride the back trails for the rest of his time, which wouldn't be long if the local law had its way or a bounty hunter got on his trail.

The smell of cooking food made him aware of how hungry he was. He got up and paced the big kitchen, his mind filled with thought. He needed to lay his hands on Pete Bolam. That man was the only means of establishing his innocence.

The inner door of the kitchen opened suddenly and Clayton whirled at the sound, his right hand flashing to the butt of his gun. The weapon seemed to leap into his grasp, and he levelled it at the man who appeared in the doorway. There was a law star pinned to the man's shirt front. Clayton cocked his gun, the muzzle gaping at the man's chest. The deputy made a movement with his right hand towards the butt of his holstered gun.

'Don't try it,' Clayton warned. 'Get 'em up high.'

The man obeyed, casting a helpless glance at Helen, who was motionless at the stove, a hand pressed to her mouth.

'Turn around,' Clayton ordered, and stepped in close, removing the man's gun. He searched for other weapons, and found a knife in a sheath, which he removed. 'Through that door over there,' he rapped. 'It's a storeroom, and when I lock you in you better be quiet. You got that?'

'Yeah.' The man nodded. 'Troy Clayton, ain't you?'

'None other. Get moving.'

The man obeyed, and Clayton checked out the storeroom when his prisoner had entered it. The room was solid, like a cell, and Clayton closed the door and dropped a thick wooden bar into position to hold it.

'You can let him out after I've left,' he said to the girl, and she turned away to continue with her chore. 'I'll fetch the other deputy in. If they're both locked up there won't be any chance of an accident.'

He went through to the front of the house, his gun still in his hand. Opening the front door, he peered out at the porch, and the second deputy looked up at him.

'Get up,' Clayton rapped. 'In here, and don't make a sound.' He showed his gun and the man sprang to his feet.

'Hey, you're Troy Clayton!' the man spluttered. He offered no resistance, and entered the house.

Clayton disarmed the man and locked him in the storeroom with his sidekick. Helen was putting the contents of the big pan on a large plate, and Clayton sat down at the table. His insides were twisting spasmodically and he was feeling faint with hunger.

He ate quickly, stuffing the food into his mouth as if there were no tomorrow. Helen finished making coffee and poured a big mugful for him. He muttered his thanks, and was silent until he had finished the meal. She sat opposite him at the table, her gaze never leaving his face. He looked at her over the rim of the mug as he swigged coffee, and shook his head slowly.

'This is a helluva business,' he remarked.

'It came about through that wild streak in you,' she said. 'I saw it in you many times before you took the plunge and went too far. You started drinking and gambling, and there was no holding you when you got started. Why couldn't you have been like Howard? He stuck to the ranch and worked like any responsible man should. But you went out and took what you wanted for your pleasure.'

'Heck, I wasn't any different from other young men.' He sounded angry. 'I didn't get into any kind of trouble. I stuck to the straight and narrow. No one was more surprised than me when I was arrested for that robbery. But I didn't do it.' He shook his head impatiently when he saw her expression. 'I ain't trying to convince you. I've given up trying to do that. There's one man in the county knows I am innocent and that's Pete Bolam, and when I catch up with him he'll tell the truth.'

'Or you'll kill him if he won't,' she said scornfully, her eyes filled with bitterness.

He pushed back his chair and got to his feet, filled with anger. 'I don't want to hear any more talk of how bad I'm supposed to be,' he rapped. 'I wanta see my pa. Then I'll get out of here and you can forget that I ever existed.'

Helen arose instantly, her face impassive. 'This way,' she said curtly, and led the way out of the kitchen.

Clayton followed her like a boy who was being punished for a misdemeanour. He was feeling guilty, when he, and only he, knew that he was innocent.

3

A knot of emotion tied itself in Clayton's chest when Helen opened the door of a bedroom and he walked in to see his father lying motionless in a bed by the window. He walked around the bed until he could see his father's face, and was shocked at the changes that had been wrought in the older man by the stress of the past seven years.

Henry Clayton had always been a big, powerful man, strong as a bull, muscular, proud of his strength even in his fifties. Now his face was creased and wrinkled, his cheeks fallen in, his eyes sunken in their sockets. There was an unhealthy pallor to his features, and his hair was wispy and grey.

'He was shot twice,' Helen said in a low tone. 'One bullet hit the side of his head just above the right ear and the second caught him in the back through the right shoulder blade. The doctor says he's on the mend, but the bullet that hit his head is causing the real trouble. Henry hasn't regained consciousness at all. The doctor thinks he will eventually, but all we can do at the moment is live in hope that he will make a complete recovery.'

'Where did it happen?' Clayton had to struggle against emotion, and his voice sounded vibrant, low pitched.

'Water Gully. He was crossing the stream, coming back from town, and someone was waiting for him in the cottonwoods on the town side.'

'Shot in the back!' Clayton clenched his hands.

'The sheriff looked into it. He found some tracks left by the ambusher and followed them until they petered out on hard ground.'

'When was he shot?'

'Three weeks ago yesterday.'

Clayton drew a deep breath and restrained it for a moment, fighting for control while angry impulses surged through his mind. He bent over the motionless figure in the bed and placed a gentle hand upon a wasted shoulder.

'Pa,' he said softly, 'I don't reckon you can hear me, but I'm back in the county and I'm gonna find who did this to you. I'm gonna do a lot of things now I'm back in this neck of the woods.'

'You're wasting your time.' Helen spoke softly. 'He can't hear you.'

'I know that!' he flashed. 'I'm making a vow, that's all, and it's one I shall keep.'

He moved away from the bed and looked out the window, which gave him a view of the big yard. There were cowboys moving all around, some mounted and riding out to start their day's work and others already busy doing chores around the place.

'I didn't get around to asking Barney Draper exactly why he doesn't work for Tented C any more,' he observed. 'I thought that old ranny would die on the spread. He was working here before I was born. Why did he quit, Helen? Do you know? When I was growing up he was more a father to me than my own father. He taught me to ride and shoot, and gave me my first horse.'

'He never did see eye to eye with Howard, and, after you'd gone, the longer they wrangled the wider the gap between them became. Then one day Howard was laying down the law about you, and Barney up and told him straight that you were more of a man than Howard could ever be. That finished Barney around here, and not even your father could get him to stay.'

'I have to go now.' Clayton was remembering that Barney was holed up on the rim of the valley, and probably getting impatient. 'I'll drop by from time to time to see how Pa makes out.'

'What are your plans?' Helen stood up to him, looking into his face and holding his gaze. 'You can't come and go as you please. You'll try it once too often and the law will get you. There's been some bad talk about you ever

57

since they figured you would come back to see your father.'

'If those two deputies I locked in the storeroom are anything to go by then Kline's men won't worry me too much. See you around, Helen.'

He left the room but paused in the doorway to take a last look at his father. His expression hardened and he shook his head. Someone was going to pay for this, he vowed. He went down the stairs, crossed to the front door, and walked out to the porch. He stood for a moment looking around at the familiar view. He had never expected to see Tented C again in this life, and a pang stabbed through him as he stepped off the porch and started across the yard. With the deputies locked in the storeroom he figured there was no reason why he should not leave openly.

As he passed a shack, the foreman's place he remembered, the door was opened and a man emerged to pull up short at the sight of a stranger. He was a hard-faced, tight-lipped range man with the obvious signs of a battler indelibly stamped on his features. His left ear was badly swollen and misshapen. A livid scar which reached from the hair line to disappear under his chin was etched down the right side of his face, and the flesh around his eyes was permanently puffed and bruised by the many hard knuckles that had been directed at him over the years.

He was solid, strong, and looked tough. Dressed in dirty range clothes, his bowed legs were clad in scarred, black bat-wing chaps. His grey shirt was open to the waist, revealing a barrel-like chest that was thickly matted with black hair. Slitted brown eyes like those of an angry bull glared out of his battered face. A holstered sixgun was suspended from a sagging cartridge-belt buckled around his thick waist.

'Who in hell are you?' he challenged, looking Clayton up and down.

'I'll ask you the same question.' Clayton did not like the man's blustering tone, and the frustration bottled up in his chest goaded him like a burr under a saddle. 'Who in hell are you?'

'I'm asking the questions.' The man's rasping voice was filled with belligerence. 'You got some business here?'

'If I have it's my business. I ain't asking what right you got to be here.'

'I'm Hoke McGee. I run this outfit. If you're looking for a job then forget it. I ain't hiring.' He glanced around with quick, furtive eyes. 'Where's your hoss? You better pile back in your saddle and light out afore I take your attitude personal. I eat a cowpoke for breakfast every day, and I ain't eaten yet!' He guffawed loudly, but there was no mirth in the sound.

'You're the foreman of Tented C?' Clayton shook his head, gazing in disbelief at this man who had taken Barney Draper's place. 'Heck, you got all the ear marks of a long rider, McGee. If you ain't a wrong 'un then I never met a cow thief before. Who set you up as foreman?'

A gleam like the flame of a fire came

to life in McGee's dark eyes. He lifted his hands, his fingers working spasmodically, as if he could already feel Clayton's flesh being mangled by them. He growled like a bear awakening from winter hibernation. His thin lips parted as he prepared to speak, but the sound of rapidly approaching hooves in the yard caught his attention and his head jerked around on his thick neck. Clayton glanced to the right and saw Barney coming in at the gateway, riding fast and leading Clayton's gelding. He raised dust in the yard and brought his horse to a slithering halt in front of McGee.

'What in hell are you doing here, Draper?' the foreman snarled. 'You forgotten what I said I'd do to you if you ever showed up around here again?'

Clayton moved forward a pace as McGee lifted his hands to grab Barney, intending to drag him out of his saddle. He grasped the butt of McGee's gun, slid it out of leather, and cocked it as he stuck the muzzle into McGee's fleshy side.

'Hold your horses,' he rasped, and the foreman froze. He turned his head to look at Clayton and the red flame in his eyes brightened to white heat.

'You sure as hell nominated yourself for big trouble,' he snarled.

'Back off before I plant another belly button in your fat gut,' Clayton told him harshly.

'Don't mess with him, Troy.' Barney spoke desperately. 'He's a man-eater, Son.'

'Not while I got a gun on him, he ain't.'

'Troy!' McGee jerked out. 'You're Troy Clayton!'

'The very same, and, mister, I don't like you. Not one little bit.' Clayton jabbed the muzzle of the gun into McGee's side and twisted it, forcing the blade of the foresight into the hard flesh. McGee backed off, raising his hands shoulder high, his fingers working convulsively.

'So you're Troy Clayton,' he said. 'The fella everyone in the county is getting all het up about. Well that don't cut no ice with me. You're a killer wanted by the law, and I got orders to drop you if you show around here.'

'Is that so?' Anger brought beads of sweat to Clayton's forehead. He uncocked the gun and thrust it deep into McGee's holster, then stepped back a couple of paces, his right hand dropping to his side. 'If you reckon you can put me down then make your play. I got you pegged for what you are, McGee, and that ain't foreman of this place. Pull your gun so I can kill you.'

'Don't do it, Troy,' Barney rapped. 'Let's get outa here. The rest of this crew are all pards of McGee, and every last one of them is stamped the same as him. Now you know why I quit.'

'Who brought them in?' Clayton watched McGee intently. 'I can't believe Pa did, not in a hundred years.'

'Howard said he needed extra muscle around the place. Your pa lost all heart in Tented C after they took you away, and he let Howard step up into the big saddle.' A note of desperation sounded in Barney's voice. 'Let's get outa here, huh, Troy?'

'When I've settled McGee.' Clayton's pale eyes glinted. 'You got orders to drop me if I ever showed up around here, huh? So what are you waiting for? You won't get a better chance than this. It must be your lucky day.'

McGee looked into Clayton's eyes, read desire and intention burning in them, and kept his hands shoulder high. He shook his head.

'It ain't the time for my play,' he said resolutely. 'You better get outa here before my boys show up. You can't fight the whole outfit, Clayton.'

'Lift your gun and work the trigger.' Frustration was burning in Clayton at white heat. 'I won't tell you a second time. Go to it, McGee.'

McGee shook his head. 'Nope. I can wait. My day will come. You better git the hell out of here while you can.'

Clayton struggled against his temper, barely managing to hold it in check. He backed off a pace and turned to take his reins from Barney. His left foot was lifting to his stirrup when a heavy hand clamped upon his shoulder, dragging him off balance.

'Now I got you!' McGee snarled.

Clayton responded with cat-like reflexes. Instead of pulling against the weight of McGee's big hand he went with the pull and ducked to the left, his movement putting the ramrod off balance. The man's heavy right fist was already flashing around in a tight arc, the knuckles aimed for Clayton's unprotected chin. But Clayton was no longer standing where McGee expected him to be. His swiftly moving body threw great pressure on McGee's grasping hand and the man was forced to release his grip or suffer a broken thumb.

Clayton dropped into a solid stance, his upper body inclined slightly forward. McGee caught his balance and came swinging back, advancing half a pace, his hands now clenched into fearsome battering clubs. The foreman was not as tall as Clayton, but solidly built, with mighty arms, and a knowledge of and experience in rough and tumble tactics.

McGee loosed a right-hand haymaker that would have broken Clayton's neck had it landed. But Clayton merely jerked his upper body backwards a few inches and the fist whistled past his chin, missing by the width of a cigarette paper. McGee was turned half around by the power of the blow, and, before he could recover, Clayton leaned in and threw his right hand in a lashing blow that had the whole weight of his body behind it. His fist swept under McGee's right arm and smacked solidly against the ramrod's jaw in a looping uppercut. McGee sagged instantly, his feet moving instinctively to take him out of range, but Clayton's fist struck again and his bunched knuckles landed on the same spot as before, right on the point of McGee's chin.

McGee paused for a moment, frozen by the cumulative effect of the two blows. His eyes rolled in their sockets, and then he went over backwards like a tree blasted by lightning. He hit the dusty yard on his shoulders and lay inert, spread-eagled on the ground, his chest rising and falling as he gasped for air.

Clayton rubbed his knuckles. His right arm was numb almost to the elbow. He looked around to find Barney sitting his horse with a look of admiration on his rugged face, and the oldster was holding his cocked sixgun, covering three men who were staring at the inert form of their foreman in disbelief.

'Get in your saddle, Troy,' Barney rasped. 'We gotta get outa here, but fast. You men, one at a time, drag your hoglegs, unload them, and toss them away as far as you can throw them.'

The men obeyed without hesitation.

Clayton swung into his saddle and gathered up his reins. He looked around, his sweeping glance taking in the whole yard, and his blue eyes narrowed when he saw Helen standing on the porch, watching intently. He turned his horse toward the gate as Barney spurred his mount and led the way out, raising dust.

When they were clear of the ranch, Clayton reined in, but Barney kept riding.

'We're still too close, Troy. McGee will send out every man he can spare to ride us down. Let's get outa the valley before we halt.'

Clayton resumed riding, his thoughts busy with what had occurred. He had plenty to mull over. His pa had been upset when his younger son had been arrested for robbery. But he hadn't made any attempt to stand by him. Bitterness assailed Clayton, and his anger increased when he considered that Howard had taken over the running of the ranch. And why had his brother brought in men like McGee? There was lawlessness in the county but that was no reason to load the crew with gunhands. And McGee had orders to shoot Troy Clayton on sight.

When they reached high ground, Clayton reined in and turned to gaze down at the spread of buildings now far below. His eyes were narrowed to mere slits as he considered, and harsh emotion ran rampant through him.

'They ain't pretty thoughts, huh, Troy?' Barney rasped. 'I tell you, I had to quit before I exploded. I didn't like anything Howard did when he took over. He always was a strange cuss, as you no doubt recall. But he took the bit between his teeth and kept running along that same trail, getting deeper into the situation he's built up.'

'Why didn't you tell me about this last night?' Clayton thumbed back his Stetson and wiped sweat from his forehead. 'I spoke to Howard this morning but didn't get any unusual impression of him. He was keen for me to ride out, and said he'd tell Kline I was here soon as he reached town. I didn't think too much about that because Howard has always been hard on me. I figured a long time ago that older brothers act that way.'

'I saw him ride out, then turn back. So he musta seen you. What are we gonna do now, Troy?'

'Have you got any ideas?' Clayton countered. 'I know what I've got to do, and I figure I've got to do it alone. But you can say your piece if you want.'

'Can't say as I have anything in mind.' Barney rubbed his chin. 'You got one helluva mess on your plate, Troy. But mebbe you better start looking for Pete Bolam. His evidence put you in prison, and if you could get him to tell the truth then folks will have to believe you were innocent.'

'That's exactly what I have in mind.' Clayton nodded. 'When was the last time you saw Bolam?'

Barney scratched his stubbled chin. 'Can't rightly recall. He ain't never been a friend of mine. But he sure disappeared from the scene mighty fast when your pa was shot. I remember thinking at the time that mebbe Pete knew something about that ambush.'

'Who did he hang around with over the past seven years? I recall he worked for Sam Robson out at Circle R — not that he did much work. He was always loafing around town with the riff-raff of the county.

'Sam Robson sold out to Hudson Brady while you was still in prison. Chuck Brady, Hudson's son, is all growed up now, and he's bossing that outfit. They call it Double B these days.'

'I recall Hudson had a son, but he was only fifteen at the time I was arrested. The Bradys have come on a fair piece in the last seven years, huh?'

'They sure have. Hudson has bought up everything he could lay his hands on.'

'So where'd he get all his money from?'

Barney shook his head. 'I guess you'll

have to ask him that. Mebbe he found a gold mine. Ten years ago he owned the freighting business, and that was all. Now he owns the general store, the livery stable, and a couple of saloons. He's got a big office on Main Street and moves in the top circle. Matt Wilson, the banker, Bill Coppard, the lawyer, and Frank Beales, who runs the newspaper, are the kind of men Brady mixes with now. The sky's the limit with Brady.'

'Is that so?' Clayton pulled a face. 'So Hudson Brady is aiming high! Mebbe he's getting his backing from the bank. But let's get back to Pete Bolam. Did he have any particular friends? I can't believe he'd pull stakes and ride out just because he figured I might come back to the county. Knowing Pete, I reckon he's lying low somewheres, waiting to see which way the wind blows.'

'You could be right. Thinking about him, I reckon he could be hiding out at Double B. He ain't no great shakes as a cowhand, but I should think he's been mighty useful to a man like Hudson Brady.'

Clayton nodded. 'I'll take a ride out that way and look around some. What about you, Barney? Those men back in town sure got tough with you. If you go back now they'll probably take up with you where they left off, and you could wind up dead.'

'I ain't goin' back to town until this business is settled one way or another.' Barney touched the bruise on the side of his head. 'They sure were playing for keeps, Troy. If you hadn't showed up when you did they would have taken me apart to get to you.'

'I ain't keen to have you riding with me.' Clayton shook his head as he considered. 'Every man in the county is gonna turn his gun against me the moment I'm seen anywhere. But I'm used to riding like that. I've been dodging lead for a long time now. But I sure wouldn't want you to join me and share in that. If you're seen with me they'll outlaw you like they did me, and there's no way back from that situation.'

'I'm sticking with you, Troy.' There was determination in the oldster's tone. 'I don't like what they did to you years ago, and they sure ain't gonna deal out any better treatment to you now. I got a bad taste in my mouth, and the only way I can get rid of it is by siding you and helping you prove your innocence.'

'Thanks, Barney. It makes me feel good to hear you talk like that. There ain't another living soul in the county feels that way about me. Even my own pa disowned me.' His pale eyes glinted. 'But they'll all sit up and take notice before we're done.'

Barney grinned. 'So we ride down Pete Bolam and make him squeal like a stuck pig, huh? You know, Troy, I'm gonna like that. I'm gonna like that a whole bunch.'

Clayton glanced around. 'We better get on the move. There were two deputies waiting at the ranch in case I showed up and I locked them in the storeroom. Helen will have turned them loose by now and I reckon they'll be after me soon as they can saddle up. But you got to promise me one thing, Barney. If there's any shooting, you duck out of it and let me handle it. I don't want anything bad happening to you. If I do succeed in proving my innocence then I'm gonna need some friends around me, and you rate top of the list.'

'The hell you say!' Barney shook his head. 'You can say what you like, Troy. I ain't wearing it. I'm in this with you whether I like it or not. Those two galoots back in town were gonna work me over real good to learn what I know about you. I got to make a stand now, and I'd rather do it with you than try to buck them alone. I know which side my bread is buttered, Son. Apart from that, a man has got to fight against injustice or he ain't any kind of a man. So let's get riding, and I don't want to hear any more gab about me ducking out if the going gets tough.'

Clayton smiled as they went on, but there was warm regard in his heart for this old man. In the past, Barney had always been there for him. As the foreman of Tented C, he had watched the two Clayton boys grow up. He had selected and broken in Troy's first horse, and taught him the rudiments of the self-sufficiency that was essential in this harsh country. But now he was out in the cold, in the wrong with the law because of his steadfastness, and Clayton vowed that, somehow, he would change all that.

4

The Double B ranch headquarters was sprawled in a bend of the wide stream that meandered across the entire county from north-west to south-east, and lay roughly twenty miles to the north of Tented C. As they rode, Clayton questioned Barney about the local situation, but learned few pertinent facts. The old man was suspicious of the businessmen in Sunset Ridge. He believed that Pete Bolam was guilty of robbery and murder, and had a low opinion of Hondo Kline and the entire law department.

They reined up on a knoll half a mile from the Double B and gazed around. A herd of white-faced steers was grazing in the middle distance, and a couple of riders were moving across the background, riding into the ranch headquarters from the north.

'Looks like a lot of work has been done on the spread since Sam Robson sold out,' Clayton observed.

'You're right. Sam never had more than one barn and one corral, but Brady is spending a whole lot of dough bringing the place up to scratch. He's bought out a couple of other ranches as well. Tom Benton, over by Dry Creek, sold out after he had a little trouble over water rights, and Bill Holder also quit. Both places went to Brady.'

'Did Brady force them out?'

'Can't say. I figure it was more like no one else would buy the spreads. Whether buyers were frightened off or not I don't know. But you know the way these things happen. It wouldn't be the first time a land shark moved in on a range and snapped it up piece by piece.'

'How do we find out if Pete Bolam is hiding here?' Clayton thumbed back his Stetson and wiped his brow. 'Neither of us can ride in and ask his whereabouts. Do you know the kind of horse Bolam rides?'

'Sure. He's had the same animal for several years. It's a bay with a chestnut-coloured head. Once you've seen that animal you couldn't mistake it for any other. A number of men have tried to buy it off Bolam but he won't sell.'

'Then if Bolam is here his horse should be in one of those corrals. Can we get closer to the spread from another direction?' Clayton studied the range. 'If we went off to the right and circled around that rise we might get in close enough to check the horses.'

'If the animal ain't here it won't tell us much. Bolam might have gone out to one of the line camps. He sure don't wanta run into you, Troy. He'll stay well clear. The trouble is, everyone in the county knows I sympathize with you. No one will wanta talk to me, and they certainly wouldn't tell me if they've seen Bolam lately.'

'If his horse ain't here we'll know he's not on the spread, and we can cast a wider loop for him.'

'If I could get to talk to Al Regan I reckon I'd learn something.' Barney looked thoughtfully at Clayton. 'Regan is the Double B cook. I've seen him sometimes when he's come into town for supplies, and he has chatted some. He's like an old woman; likes a bit of gossip. He's told me about some of the improvements being done on the ranch, and he don't mind talking about Brady. You reckon I could ride in there and try to see Regan?'

'I wouldn't give much for your chances if they figure out what you're really doing there.' Clayton shook his head. 'I guess you might have gotten away with it last week, but now they know I'm back in the county they'll be watching points. Let's work our way in as close as we can and you look out for Bolam's horse.'

They moved back off the knoll and followed the fall of the range, riding to the right. Rising ground came between them and the Double B, concealing the clustered buildings. Clayton spotted an arroyo which cut along in the general direction he wished to go. They entered it and continued, emerging shortly to find themselves looking at Double B from the east side. The nearest corral was only fifty yards away.

'Let's hope we don't get spotted out here,' Barney observed. 'Ranchers don't like being spied on.'

Clayton smiled. 'Over the past seven years I got used to going wherever I wanted, and nobody managed to stop me.'

'This is home range, remember.' Barney shook his head. He produced a pair of binoculars from a saddle bag and adjusted them to his eyes. Clayton watched their surroundings while the oldster studied the spread. 'Nope. I don't see hide nor hair of Bolam's bronc,' he said shortly. 'If he is hiding out here he ain't likely to leave the horse where it can be spotted. It's possible he's gone out to one of Brady's line camps for a spell.'

'I'll find him soon.' Clayton tensed

when he caught sight of movement off to the right. His head jerked round to cover the area and he saw three riders appearing on a crest. They came forward at a canter. 'We got company,' he said.

Barney twisted in his saddle, then groaned under his breath. 'That's company all right. It's Hudson Brady hisself. Never rides alone these days. They're a couple of gunnies siding him — Joe Quirk and Speck Hansen.'

Clayton sat motionless, holding his reins in his left hand. His right hand rested lightly on his right thigh, conveniently close to the butt of his holstered gun.

'I can see the man in the middle is Hudson Brady,' he said shortly. 'He's put on a lot of weight since I saw him last.'

'In the old days he worked hard building up his business, but these days he sits in that office of his in town and lounges around all the time. His work is handled by a manager, and his son runs this spread.'

The riders came up fast, raising dust, and reined in facing Clayton and Barney. Clayton eyed Brady intently, waiting to find out how the man greeted him.

Hudson Brady was solid-looking, around fifty years old. He had a great wide forehead and a fleshy face that was dominated by a long, curving nose perched above a thin-lipped mouth. His eyes were smoke-grey, filled with an impersonal expression that gave one the impression that he was not really interested in his fellow men. Dressed in expensive range clothes, he wore a cream-coloured Stetson decorated with a silver band that glinted in the sunlight.

The black stallion Brady sat astride was a magnificent animal with a spirited temperament. Its eyeballs rolled as it champed on the bit and continually pulled and shook its head while Brady fought it all the way with unsympathetic hands. The horse needed a lot of strength to ride, and Brady was up to the task, holding it in with the same contempt he felt for everyone and everything.

'What have we here?' he demanded in a nasal tone. 'The whole county is out looking for Troy Clayton and he's sitting large as life on my doorstep. What are you doing here? Looking for a job?'

Clayton remained silent for a moment, trying to gauge the man's true attitude from his words. Hudson's face was like a mask. There was no expression. But his grey eyes sparkled coldly, as if he found amusement in the situation.

'I'm back in the county to set the record straight,' Clayton said at length. 'I figure it's time the truth came out.'

'Is that so? Then what took you so long? If you're interested, I never believed you were guilty. It looked like a put-up job to me. You were still wet behind the ears when they railroaded

84

you. They forced you into what you've become.'

Surprise trickled through Clayton but he did not let the revelation affect his alertness. His gaze encompassed all three men, and he could see that the two gunnies were tense, ready for action. Both men were strangers to him, and they looked like a couple of leashed dogs awaiting the order to attack.

'From what I've heard about Troy Clayton, I reckon he's no good,' one of the men said when Clayton's gaze rested on him. He was a tall, thin individual, dressed in a black store suit and a flat-crowned plains hat. Crossed cartridge-belts encircled his slim waist and the pearl-handled butts of twin pistols protruded from the tied-down holsters on his thighs. His dark eyes were glittering, entirely devoid of emotion.

'Who asked for your opinion, Speck?' Hudson demanded. 'You reckon you could take care of Clayton, huh? Your professional pride is on the line here, ain't it? Well, from what I've heard about Troy Clayton, I reckon you wouldn't clear leather before he knocked you outa your saddle. That goes for you, too, Joe. Both of you sit quiet and you might learn something.' He grinned wickedly at Clayton, who remained unperturbed. 'I'd back you to handle both these men with your eyes closed and one hand tied behind your back.'

'Two-bit gunnies don't bother me,' Clayton opined. 'What's on your mind, Brady?'

'Why should I have anything on my mind?'

'You must have or you would have turned your gunhawks loose on me the minute I was spotted. Unless you are afraid you might lose them if they tried. Mebbe you'd like to see who is fastest around here, huh? You wouldn't want slower guns guarding you. I figure you always go for the best.'

Brady laughed. 'I reckon you are as

cool as they say, Clayton. I could use a man like you, if you could prove your innocence. You got an idea where to start looking for your proof?'

'If I am innocent then the man who said he saw me commit the robbery had to be lying.'

'Pete Bolam. Yeah. I guess that's it in a nutshell. But Pete ain't been around for a couple of weeks. He took off north on a long trip. Reckoned his mother was dying. But to me it sure looks like you spooked him. He wouldn't be too keen to meet up with you, considering the water that's flowed under the bridge. What about Frank Butler's murder? They reckon that was the first thing you did when you got outa prison.'

'What for would I wanta kill old Frank? For his money?' Clayton shook his head. 'Hell, no! What Frank had didn't amount to a can o' beans. If I was desperate for money I would have hit the bank, or even dropped on to you. Your freight line was more profitable than Frank's saddlery. Is that or ain't it a solid fact?'

Brady nodded. 'Yeah. I guess you're right at that. Why didn't Kline think of it at the time? But they found your knife in Butler's shop. There was bloodstains on it, along with your name. Everyone knew that knife by sight, and Bill Tobin, the storekeep in those days, swore he sold it to you just a coupla days before the murder.'

'Knife?' Clayton shook his head, his eyes glittering. 'I never owned a knife.'

'Ain't that the gospel, Draper? Didn't they find the murder knife, which had Troy's name on it?' Brady turned his cold eyes on Barney, who started as if awakening from a deep sleep, being intent on what was being said, following every word with great interest.

'Yeah, that's what they said,' Barney agreed. 'But I told everyone at the time that Troy never carried a knife, and wasn't the type to use one.'

Clayton shook his head. Impatience flared through him, and hopelessness.

How could he hope to prove his innocence? Whoever set him up had done a real good job. Nothing had been left to chance.

'Sitting here chatting about it ain't gonna prove anything,' he rasped. 'If you've got anything to say to me, Brady, then spit it out. I ain't got time for beating around the bush.'

Brady shook his head. 'I just want you to know that I'm not an enemy. There'll be some in the county who might tell you otherwise. But I have a lot of enemies around here, most of them against me through jealousy. I hope you find what you're looking for. You can take my word for it that Pete Bolam ain't here at Double B. Mebbe you should take a look around town for him. He could be hiding out close to home, waiting for someone to kill you so he can come out into the open again.'

Clayton was startled by the information, and his right hand jerked a little towards his gun butt as Brady dragged on his reins and pulled his horse away. But Brady was leaving. He set spurs into the flanks of his big black and the high-spirited animal cavorted and reared, then surged forward past Clayton, heading in a dead run for the nearby ranch.

The two gunnies were taken by surprise by Brady's action, and set off in frantic pursuit, casting hostile glances at Clayton in passing. Clayton turned his horse as they went by, keeping his face to them. Dust floated around him.

'If that don't beat all!' he said. 'I didn't know what to expect from Brady when he rode up, and he sure surprised me. What do you make of it, Barney?'

'Don't trust him,' Barney replied. 'Me, I'd rather trust a rattler. But he was only talking facts, Troy. Anybody with an ounce of savvy can work out that you are innocent. I reckon Hudson Brady has got an axe to grind somewhere in the county, and already he's figuring that you're the man to handle whatever he's got in mind. He'll use you if he can, then toss you to the sheriff.'

'Do we accept his word that Bolam ain't on the ranch? And did he tell the truth when he figured Bolam might be holed up in town?'

Barney shrugged and grimaced. 'Like I told you, Pete Bolam dropped out of sight unexpectedly, and I ain't heard even a whisper about where he might have gone to ground. If he is still in town then we got to try and work out where he's hiding.'

'Has he got any special friends?'

'I don't think he's got a single friend in the whole county, but some people would hide him if the price was right. Let me think about that, Troy. We could do worse than head back to Sunset Ridge. Riding around the range is only gonna tire us out.'

Clayton saw the logic in Barney's words but still hesitated, impatient to get on and find the man who had railroaded him. He had reckoned it would be a simple matter to find Bolam and make him tell the truth. But he was beginning to realize that it was more complicated than that. There was also the murder of Frank Butler to be unravelled. He needed a lot of help to find a hot trail, and being out in the middle of nowhere could only hold him back.

'Let's go back to town,' he decided. 'I reckon, if all else fails, I can drop in on Hondo Kline and have a talk with him.'

'Are you crazy?' Barney shook his head. 'If you rouse up Kline he'll have every man in the county out after you.'

'That might be to the good, if Bolam happens to be one of them. Then I might be able to drop on to him.' Clayton was still watching the departing riders, and when they disappeared among the distant ranch buildings he turned his horse and sent the animal at a canter in the direction of Sunset Ridge.

'There's a lot about your problems that don't add up, Troy,' Barney said after thinking for a long spell. 'I allus had a hunch that Hudson Brady was back of your troubles, for reasons known only to hisself. But listening to him back there, I don't know so much. Unless he is more devious than I gave him credit for. But the only way to look at this is to pick out who could have been behind it if Brady isn't guilty.'

'I know what you mean but that's too deep for me.' Clayton shook his head. 'I wouldn't know where to start looking for someone who's just a shadow in the background.'

'I don't reckon it is so hard. Nobody does anything for nothing in this world. There's got to be a reason why you were set up, and if you find it you'll be looking at the man who framed you.'

'Sure. So what reason could there be? I can't think of anyone who wanted me out of the way. And wouldn't it have been easier just to shoot me than set me up? Heck, I was just a raw kid in those days, and nothing about that frame-up makes any sense. I wasn't old enough to have made an enemy anywhere.'

'Yeah. That's what bugs me.' Barney sighed and shook his head. 'Mebbe you didn't make an enemy, but you sure enough had one. Whoever set you up didn't spare an effort. He brought in Pete Bolam, remember, and when you came out of prison he had Frank Butler murdered to throw the blame on you. What about that, Troy? Bill Tobin stood up at the inquest on Butler and swore he sold you the murder weapon a couple of days before Butler was killed.'

'Is Tobin still in town?' Clayton asked quickly.

Barney shook his head. 'He sold up and pulled out when Brady took over the store. They said Brady paid way over the odds to get the business.'

'So there were two men here who lied about me!' Clayton set his teeth into his bottom lip. 'This business gets worse instead of better. But once I get hold of Bolam I reckon to find the truth.'

They had been riding away from Double B for at least two hours, and Clayton kept throwing occasional glances along their back trail. He saw nothing suspicious for a long time, until a glint of sunlight on metal caught his keen eyes and he faced his front and urged his horse into a fast canter.

'We got company behind, Barney,' he said grimly. 'Let's get moving. Pull ahead of me and keep going. I'll see you at your shack in town if we have to split up.'

The oldster stiffened but did not turn. 'Got any idea who it is?' he demanded. 'Could be those two snakes, Quirk and Hansen. That's the sort of thing Brady would do; lull your suspicions and then send a couple of gunnies to shoot you in the back.'

'I'll drop back at the next ridge,' Clayton said.

'Someone is following our tracks and making an effort to remain out of sight,' Barney agreed. 'Could it be Pete Bolam? That's the kind of trick Brady might pull. Bolam is scared of you, but he wouldn't hesitate to put a bullet in your back if he got half a chance.'

Barney suddenly cried out in pain, and, as he slid sideways out of his saddle, the vicious crack of a distant rifle sounded behind them. They were travelling at a fast clip but Clayton reacted instantly. He pulled his rifle from its saddle boot and sprang to the ground as he jerked the gelding to a halt. The echoing reports of the shot were blasted out by more shots, and he heard the whine of slugs passing close to his head as he ran back to where Barney was lying.

To his great relief, Clayton found that Barney was only slightly hurt. Blood was showing on the upper sleeve of the old man's left arm.

'Get into cover, Troy,' Barney gasped. 'Don't give 'em a chance to draw a bead on you. Looks like they're gonna play this for keeps, huh?'

Clayton dropped flat, slitting his eyes against the glare of the sun to search the area of their back trail. He saw two riders moving from left to right along a crest about one hundred yards distant, and, even as he picked them out, two more appeared on the crest, turned left, and moved fast in an encircling movement. His eyes glinted.

'Four of them,' he said. 'They sure mean business. Can you get up and move out, Barney?'

'Stop trying to nursemaid me,' the oldster retorted. 'I was smelling gun-smoke before you were born. I'm gonna stay right here until they get here, and then we'll see who comes off best.'

Clayton shook his head, aware that he would only waste breath if he tried to talk Barney into running. Jacking a brass-bound cartridge into the breech of his rifle, he laid the sights against the foremost of the riders moving left to right. He fired without seeming to aim, and flat echoes chased across vast space. Barney twisted a little, grunting in pain, and lifted his head to watch. When one of the distant riders pitched out of his saddle he uttered a hoarse chuckle.

'No need to wonder if you learned anything I tried to teach you when you was young,' he said. 'Give 'em hell, Troy.'

Clayton drew a bead on one of the two riders moving to the left, restrained his breathing and fired. His slitted eyes watched unblinkingly, and moments later his target threw his arms wide, slumped forward over the neck of his horse, then fell from his saddle in a lifeless heap. The other two riders disappeared back beyond the ridge.

Barney chuckled. 'That taught them some respect,' he said. 'Heck I wish I was still young, Troy. What a team we'd make.'

'Let me take a look at your arm,' Clayton responded. He laid aside his rifle and checked the oldster's wound. 'Tore some flesh off, that's all,' he said.

'I told you it was nothing.' Barney pushed himself to his feet. Despite his words his face was pale with shock. Clayton helped him to his horse.

'Come on. Back into your saddle and head for town. Looks like you'll need the doctor. I'll stick around here for a spell and try conclusions with these gunnies.'

He helped Barney into his saddle and smacked the horse across the rump.

'Make sure you do come and look me up in town,' Barney called as his mount bore him swiftly away.

Clayton rode more slowly, watching his back trail. He crossed a ridge, dropping out of sight of those behind him, and rode a dozen yards to the right before swinging out of his saddle. He trailed his reins and the horse immediately lowered its head and began to graze. Taking his rifle, he went back to the crest and hunkered down out of sight, removing his tall-crowned Stetson and levering a shell into the breech of his long gun. He studied all approaches, looking for dust and movement, certain that his pursuers had not departed.

He did not have long to wait. A

movement on the back trail warned him of company, and a moment later two riders appeared, moving unhurriedly, obviously now content to follow tracks. Clayton figured the men were Quirk and Hansen, but soon changed his mind. As they drew nearer he saw that they looked like ordinary cowpokes, and apparently ready for action. They had to be Double B riders. They were riding alertly, talking little and watching their surroundings.

Clayton observed them ascending the ridge, and when they reached the crest they reined in quickly and gazed around. He realized that they had spotted his diverging trail, and both men turned in his direction, immediately seeing his horse. Clayton arose, rifle levelled, and the men froze, their faces impassive as he walked towards them.

'Looking for trouble, huh?' he demanded, halting a couple of yards to their right. 'Get rid of your guns, and bear in mind that I'm looking for an excuse to plug you.' He waited until they had complied. 'Now get out of your saddles, and stick your hands up. I'm dangerous when I smell gunsmoke.'

The men dismounted without hesitation, standing with their hands shoulder high and watching him intently. Clayton glanced around. The range was seemingly deserted and heavy silence pressed in around them.

'Who sent you after me?' he demanded. 'You ride for Double B, don't you?'

'Sure. We thought youse were rustlers.' The smaller of the two men grinned uncertainly, showing stained, broken teeth. His face was small and sharp-featured. He looked like a human rat, and his manner was furtive. Clayton read the signs of a paid gunhand about him despite his appearance.

'We been getting trouble from rustlers,' the other said. 'We got into the habit of shooting first and asking questions afterwards.'

'It's a good thing for you I don't follow the same rule,' Clayton observed. 'There was just two of us riding along minding our own business. I don't reckon anyone looked less like rustlers.'

'Well that's how we had it figured.' The smaller man sounded sullen. His dark eyes watched Clayton intently. 'What for are you riding Double B range? You ain't got no business with the ranch. Strangers ain't welcome. They spell trouble. We got our orders. And what are you gonna do about it? You're Troy Clayton. You gonna hand us over to the sheriff?'

'So you know who I am.' Clayton nodded. 'Have you ever set eyes on me before?'

'Nope. But I've heard about you.'

'That ain't the same thing.' Impatience sounded in Clayton's tone. 'Now you know who I am you better tell me your names, just in case I have to bury you. I can't leave your kind of trash above ground.'

'I'm Deke Hayman,' said the smaller

man. 'And this is Hank Edlin. You ain't got no call to kill us. We wasn't shooting to kill.'

'It didn't look that way to me.' Clayton thumbed his hat back off his eyes. 'So what am I gonna do about you two? If I turn you loose you'll come after me, and I don't need you crowding me. I reckon the only thing I can do is shoot you.'

The men accepted his words as gospel. The taller one backed off a step, eyes expressing fear. Clayton had no intention of shooting them in cold blood, but they were judging him by reputation, and expected the worst.

'Is Pete Bolam at Double B?' he demanded. 'If you speak up you just might save your lives.'

'Pete ain't been around for a couple of weeks,' Hayman said. 'He heard his mother is dying, and lit out north to see her.'

'That's the story, huh? But I'll catch up with Pete.'

The sound of approaching hoofs

came to his ears then and he glanced over his shoulder to see a group of riders galloping towards him. He recognized the obese figure of the sheriff, Hondo Kline, in the lead, and turned to run for his horse. He sprang into the saddle and hit a dead run instantly. The gelding loved a chase, and seemed to fly over the rough ground.

Clayton hunched himself in the saddle, his teeth clenched, as shooting erupted. Slugs whined perilously close around him and he lit out fast for other parts. This was the kind of progress he did not need.

5

Clayton rode at a gallop until he reached the nearest ridge. Shooting hammered continuously behind him but he was untouched by the flying lead, and the attack ceased when a crest intervened between him and his pursuers. He turned the horse to the right and rode for the next crest, and shooting resumed temporarily when his pursuers sighted him again. But he was better mounted than any of them, and quickly drew out of gun range. He settled the gelding into a mile-eating gallop and concentrated on putting distance between himself and the posse.

He wondered how a posse could have got out of town so fast. Howard had said he would inform Kline of his presence in the county, but there hadn't been time for them to appear on Double B range.

He glanced back over his shoulder and spotted the pursuers a long way back. He grinned. Having ridden out from town, and probably at a fast pace, the posse's mounts were tired, while his gelding was comparatively fresh. He settled down to ride seriously, mulling over what he had learned.

He did not understand Hudson Brady. The man had seemed friendly, but as soon as he had reached Double B he had sent four gunnies out to hunt him down. He spotted Barney's trail ahead, and, an hour later, saw the old man plodding steadily towards Sunset Ridge. He halted and dismounted to give the gelding a breather, dropping to ground to watch his back trail. There was now no sign of pursuit, and he remounted and went on at a faster pace to overhaul Barney.

He caught up with the oldster just before they sighted town, and when he saw Barney's features he was filled with concern. Barney grinned a welcome, but his face was lined with agony and he looked completely wasted.

'Barney, what's wrong?' he demanded.

The old man shook his head. When he spoke his voice was low-pitched, and he didn't seem to have enough energy to hold himself erect in the saddle. Clayton looked at the wound in Barney's left arm, and was concerned to see how much blood the man was losing.

'Hold up,' he commanded. 'You're losing too much blood.'

'I'm all right, I tell you.' Barney shook his head and kept riding. 'If I stop now I won't get going again, and I need to see the doc. There's something not right about my arm.'

'The bullet did more damage than I figured,' Clayton said. 'Stop now, Barney, or you'll likely bleed to death.'

When it seemed that Barney was determined to ride on, Clayton reached out and grabbed the oldster's reins. The horse stopped obediently and Barney slid sideways out of the saddle. Clayton only just managed to grab the oldster to save him from a heavy fall. He eased Barney to the ground and stepped down from his saddle, checking his surroundings before bending over the oldster. There was no sign of the posse.

Barney's wound, which was in the upper left arm, was bleeding heavily, and Clayton ripped off the blood-soaked sleeve and used it as a tourniquet. He managed to staunch the bleeding, and shook his head as he lifted Barney gently and placed him face down across the saddle. He mounted and rode on, leading Barney's horse, and when he crossed the next ridge he saw the main street of Sunset Ridge before him.

Barney had regained his senses by the time Clayton rode into town. The old man tried to push himself erect and slid off his horse. Clayton picked him up and sat him in the saddle.

'You all right, Barney?' he demanded.

'Sure thing.' The oldster grinned weakly. 'What in hell you done to my arm? It's throbbing like a kick from a mule.'

'I had to stop the bleeding. You lost a lot of blood. Is Frank Amos still the doctor here?'

'Yeah. You know where he lives. But you can't ride in with me, Troy. Kline would welcome you with open arms.'

Clayton moved on again, leading Barney's horse. The old man was reeling in his saddle, almost losing his balance with every step the horse took.

'Kline ain't in town.' Clayton explained what had happened on the range. 'The posse is a long ways back, if they continued after me. I got time to see you're all right before I pull out again. There were ten men in that posse so I reckon there can't be many gun-toters left in town. Let's get you to the doctor.'

He felt strange riding into town openly in daylight, and looked around with interest as they continued to the doctor's house. There were people on the main street, but no one seemed to

109

take an interest in them. Clayton saw that there had been little change in the town over the past seven years. He reined in at the hitching rail in front of the doctor's house and wrapped his reins around it. His alertness was at full power as he helped Barney out of the saddle and half carried him to the door of the house.

A woman opened the door in response to Clayton's heavy knocking, and she gasped in alarm at the gory appearance that Barney presented.

'Come inside quickly,' she urged. 'Frank isn't here at the moment, but he's trained me in simple doctoring over the years. How did this happen, Barney?'

'Someone got careless with a gun,' Barney said weakly.

Clayton remained silent. He helped Barney into the doctor's treatment room and sat him down at a table. Mrs Amos, a tall, thin woman with white hair, quickly removed the tourniquet and examined the wound.

'You're mainly suffering from loss of blood, Barney,' she said. 'You should have come to see Frank sooner.'

'We got here soon as we could,' Clayton said, and she looked at him intently, holding his gaze.

'You're Troy Clayton,' she observed.

'That's a fact.' He nodded.

'You'd better move your horse from out front. The town has been like a fort ever since Sheriff Kline figured you might ride in. Put your horses in Frank's barn behind the house and use the back door when you return. I'll unbolt it for you.'

'Thanks.' Clayton departed and took the horses along the alley at the side of the house. The town still looked quiet, and he did not think anyone would know his horse by sight.

He put the horses in the small stable on the back lots, and, as he turned to leave, a rider came up and dismounted outside. He glanced out the doorway and saw the doctor stepping down from his saddle. Frank Amos was in his early

111

sixties, tall and thin, but not frail. His years of riding the county by night and day in all weathers had toughened him. His lean face was grizzled and his hair was white, but he looked like a man who could win an argument with a maddened bull.

'Troy Clayton!' he exclaimed when Clayton showed himself. 'This is a surprise. To what do I owe the pleasure of this meeting? I must say you're looking healthy. Not needing my professional services, are you?

'No, Doc. Barney Draper is in the house. He stopped a bullet with his left arm and it's been bleeding badly.'

'I heard early this morning that Barney rode out with you last night. And now he's been shot. That should be a warning to anyone who might figure to ride with you. You're a dangerous man to be close to, Troy.'

'I'll take care of your horse, Doc,' Clayton said easily, 'while you go in and take a look at Barney.'

'Sure. And you better come into the

house by the back door. If you're spotted on the street they'll lay siege to this place, and any number of people might get hurt in the resultant shoot-out.'

'Thanks, Doc.' Clayton busied himself with the doctor's grey, and when he went to the back door it was ajar. Entering, he found himself in the kitchen. Mrs Amos was there, making coffee.

'Come right in, Troy,' she said. 'I expect you'd like some coffee. I've given Barney a big dose of whisky. He'll be all right if he rests up. You shouldn't have taken him with you, you know.' There was mild reproof in her tone.

Clayton explained how Barney happened to be riding with him.

'If I'd left him in town the sheriff's hard cases would have beaten him badly to learn about me,' he said grimly.

'Then you must put him somewhere safe until this present trouble has ended. He's too old to go riding around.'

'I'm aware of that, Ma'am. Mebbe I'd better get out of here now, before Barney can tag along again. But I'd hate anything bad to happen to him just because he knows me. You must know he ain't done anything wrong in his whole life.'

'Frank will probably keep him here in the sick room for a few days, and he won't let any of Kline's men near him. Have some coffee before you leave. Are you hungry? I can soon get some food for you.'

'I'll have coffee, that's all, thank you. But you know it's against the law to help a fugitive, don't you?'

'You know us better than that,' she retorted. 'We keep open house here. Everyone is welcome. But Frank has spoken about you many times, Troy, and he's never even hinted that he thinks you're guilty.'

Clayton leaned a shoulder against the doorpost and drank his coffee. Doc

Amos came into the kitchen and washed his hands.

'Barney will be all right now,' he said. 'I've given him a sedative because he's been insisting that he's got to leave with you. I'll keep him here for a few days, Troy. But you better make yourself scarce.'

'I'm concerned that Kline's hard cases might beat him up to try and make him talk about me,' Clayton said.

'They won't get their hands on him.' There was a grim note in the doctor's voice. 'What are you planning now you're back in the county?'

'I'm gonna prove my innocence, Doc.'

'That's easier said than done. You need to get hold of Pete Bolam to have any kind of a chance.'

'You get around a lot in your job. Do you know where Bolam is likely to be hiding out?'

'He was working out at the Double B until he suddenly dropped out of sight. For what it's worth, I always thought he committed perjury at your trial, Troy. But if he set you up then he was acting on someone's orders, and, now you're back to prove your innocence, it's possible that Bolam has been murdered to silence him. Have you thought of that?'

'It's crossed my mind. I'm going out now to look for Bolam. If I don't find him then I'm in big trouble.'

'You could do worse than speak to Madge Austin. She's seen a lot of Bolam during the last couple of years, and when I saw her a couple of days ago she was complaining about the way Bolam cheated her out of some money. She might know a bit more about Bolam's business, and it's likely she'll be feeling spiteful towards him right now, which might benefit you.'

'Thanks, Doc. Where will I find her?'

'She's the clerk at the hotel. Hudson Brady owns the place now, but there's no love lost between them. Leave your horse in my barn until you're ready to ride out, and watch out for Slick Porter.

His pride was hurt by the way you handled him last night, and that's quite apart from the broken jaw you gave him. He ain't a man to overlook any transgression, and when I attended him he was making all manner of threats against you.'

'I also shot a man last night. How's he doing?'

'He'll live. Be careful how you toss lead around town, Troy. It won't help you if an innocent bystander is killed.'

'I never draw my gun unless I have to,' Clayton said quietly. 'Before I leave, Doc, tell me about my father. Is his life in danger?'

'Not as far as I can tell.' Amos shook his head. 'There is talk that Pete Bolam dry-gulched him. Bolam sure has got a lot to answer for, huh? Don't worry about your father, Troy. I figure he'll suddenly open his eyes one day, and when he does he'll be as good as new.'

Clayton nodded. 'Thanks, Doc. That makes me feel good. Take care of Barney, huh?'

'Sure thing. But watch your step. Have you seen Howard since you came back?'

'Yeah. We had words out at Tented C this morning. He told me to get out of the county, and I figure he came into town and told Kline I was at the ranch. The sheriff turned up at Double B as I was leaving there, and his posse started shooting on sight.'

'It's a bad business.' Amos shook his head. 'I hope you can prove your innocence, Troy.'

'So do I, Doc.' Clayton grimaced and departed.

He left the house by the back door, pausing outside to check the loads in his pistol. Then he crossed the back lots to the rear of the hotel. He was relieved to learn that some folks in the county thought that he might be innocent.

A saddle horse was standing with trailing reins by the rear entrance to the hotel, looking as if it had recently travelled far and fast. Clayton patted it in passing, and frowned when he realized that the rider had not put the animal in the livery barn. He paused as a thought struck him, and went back to the animal to check its brand. He moistened his lips when he saw Double B on its rump, and wondered who owned it.

Entering the hotel by the back door, he moved silently along a corridor to a door at the far end, which, he knew, gave access to the front of the building. Opening the door a fraction, he peered into the lobby, and was relieved to see that it was deserted except for a man seated behind the reception desk.

Easing his gun in its holster, Clayton went to the desk. The man looked up at him, frowning.

'Say, where did you spring from?' he demanded. 'I didn't see you come in.'

'I used the back door. Where's Madge Austin. Ain't she the clerk here?'

'She is, but she just quit. And I got to look after the place till Brady gets back. It's a helluva thing! Pete Bolam rides in and there's a humdinger of a row between him and Madge. She threw the book at him.' He dropped a hand to the register lying on the desk and grinned. 'Hit him on the head with it. Bolam yelled and cursed some, and Madge was fit to be tied. But all the same, in the end she went off with him. They're heading for San Francisco, so I gathered. What do you want with Madge? If you need a room, I can handle that.'

'I don't need a room. I need to talk to Madge. Where can I find her? Does she live in the hotel?'

'Nope. She's got a room at Ma Gibson's boarding-house along the street. You can't miss it. Just past the bank. It's got a sign up outside.'

'Whose horse is standing at the back door?'

'Dunno. I didn't know there was one there.'

'It's got the Double B brand on it.'

'Must be Bolam's. He came in the back door when he arrived.'

'How long ago did he leave?'

'Must be all of thirty minutes. Him and Madge plan to catch the west-bound stage this afternoon.'

Clayton turned on his heel and left the hotel by the front door. Pausing on the sidewalk, he looked around with a keen gaze. There were not many people on the street, and he failed to spot Bolam anywhere. He went along the sidewalk, watching his surroundings. The law office was on the opposite side of the street, almost facing the bank, and he was thinking of taking to the back lots again when a group of riders swung into the street and raised dust all the way to the law office.

Clayton stepped unhurriedly into the nearest alley mouth and stood in its shadow. He saw the obese figure of the sheriff, Hondo Kline, dismount heavily and stomp on to the sidewalk opposite. The sheriff's booming voice echoed across the street when he called to the jailer inside the office. Kline turned to face his posse. He hitched up his sagging gun-belt and it immediately slipped down his fat stomach again. He was sweating profusely. His face was covered with a sheen of moisture. The possemen looked hot and tired, their mounts weary, standing with drooping heads.

'Go get fresh hosses and we'll ride out again,' Kline said raspingly. 'You wanta catch Clayton, don't you?'

'I ain't riding out again today,' a man said, and wheeled his mount away from the law office. 'You're chasing shadows, Sheriff. You got Troy Clayton on your mind.'

One by one the possemen turned away and departed. Some went on along the street to the livery barn, but several dropped off at the nearest saloon and trooped inside. Kline stood watching them, his fleshy face brooding. A tall deputy emerged from the law office and joined the sheriff. He had a bandage around his lower face, and Clayton guessed he was looking at Slick Porter. A law star was glinting on the man's chest.

Kline's voice echoed around the street, and Clayton heard every word the sheriff said.

'We had tough luck, Slick. Missed him at Tented C so we went on to Double B. There was shooting going on this side of the spread and we rode in as it was ending. I saw Troy Clayton plain as I'm looking at you. But he was a long ways off, and he's got a powerful piece of hossflesh under his saddle. We chased after him but he left us standing. The last we saw of him he looked to be heading for town. Have you set eyes on him?'

'If I had he'd be dead or in jail by now.' Porter was having trouble talking and his words were slurred. 'He took me by surprise last night, but the next time we meet I won't make any mistake.'

'I figure the next time you face him he'll kill you,' Kline retorted. 'I'm gonna get me a beer. And you don't want to sit skulking in the office. Move around the town and keep your eyes skinned for Clayton. He came back this way, and he's looking for Pete Bolam. Watch Bolam and you'll drop on to Clayton.'

'Where the hell is Bolam?' Porter snarled. 'He ain't been seen for a couple of weeks.'

'I heard at Double B that he's leaving the county for his health. Hudson told him to make himself scarce till Clayton's been taken. You ain't doin' your job properly, Slick. If Clayton came back to town you should know about it. And while you're at it, check Doc Amos out. I heard that Barney Draper stopped a slug out at Double B and will likely need to see the doc. Draper is another who can lead you to Clayton. Watch him closely. Clayton will be checking on him from time to time, or I miss my guess.'

Clayton watched the sheriff step off the sidewalk and shamble like a bear through the dust of the street to the nearest saloon. Porter turned and reentered the law office despite the sheriff's orders. Clayton checked out the street again. There was little movement anywhere. He turned and went along the alley to the back lots, walking past the rear of the bank and turning into another alley. When he reached the street, the law office was twenty yards to his right, and he looked to the left and saw a sign advertising Ma Gibson's boarding-house.

Clayton drew his gun and checked its loads, then blew some dust from its barrel. If his information was correct then Pete Bolam was here with Madge Austin. He settled the gun back in its holster and walked casually to the door of the boarding-house. A pulse was beating vibrantly in his right temple.

A woman appeared from an inner room when Clayton entered the house. She was plump and motherly looking, aged around fifty.

'Can I help you?' she asked, looking

him up and down. 'Are you wanting a room?'

'No thanks, Ma'am. I need to talk to Madge Austin, and they told me at the hotel that I'd find her here.'

'Madge is up in her room. She's packing to go on a trip. I'll get her for you.'

'I'd rather see her in her room.' Clayton moved to the flight of stairs. 'Just tell me which room.'

'I don't usually let men up into the rooms.'

'I'm a cousin of Madge. I got bad news.'

'Her father?' The woman looked concerned. 'Madge heard he was ill. Her room is first on the right.'

'Thanks.' Clayton turned and ascended the stairs. He paused on the upper landing to look around, then approached the door on the right. Removing his Stetson, he pressed his ear against the door but heard nothing. He drew his gun and cocked it, then grasped the door handle and turned it gently. The door opened a fraction and he steeled himself for action, then thrust the door open and stepped inside to halt on the threshold.

A woman was standing by the bed, putting clothes into a carpetbag. She looked up at his entrance and instinctively moved back a step in alarm, her hands lifting to her breast. Fear showed on her face and she opened her mouth as if to scream.

'Don't make a sound, Madge,' Clayton said softly. 'I only want to ask you a few questions.

'About Pete?' Her voice was little more than a whisper. 'You're Troy Clayton, ain't you?'

'Where is Pete?' He could see at a glance that Bolam was not in the room. 'He was with you at the hotel.'

'You're planning to kill Pete.' Her voice rose slightly as fear took hold of her. 'What's he ever done to you? I've got to leave town because you're after Pete.'

'Where is he?' Clayton holstered his gun and half turned to close the door. He leaned a broad shoulder against the door and waited for Madge to tell him . . .

6

'I don't know where Pete is.' Madge Austin spoke nervously. She was a tall, thin woman in her late thirties, with a long face that had lost its first bloom of youth. Her yellow hair was set in a sophisticated style, all curls and ringlets, and looked as if it had been dyed too often. There was a network of fine wrinkles around her blue eyes. Her cheeks were fleshless, the skin drawn tightly across her facial bones. She looked at Clayton with consternation in her eyes, and her hands shook as she took in the tension about him, the eagerness he evinced as he awaited her words. When she did not speak he moved impatiently.

'You're lying, Madge.' His tone was intense. 'Pete was with you when you left the hotel half an hour ago. You're getting ready to leave with him on the afternoon stage. So where is he?'

'You'll kill him if I tell you!'

Clayton shook his head. 'That's the last thing I wanta do. Seven years ago, because Pete told lies about me, they sent me to prison. I need him to put things straight with the law.'

'Then you'll kill him,' she insisted.

'I'll do a deal with you. Tell me where he is and I won't kill him, unless he pushes it with me. I need Pete badly, and I'll let him live if he'll come up with the truth.'

She looked at him for moments that seemed to stretch into an eternity, then sighed and shook her head, as if mentally discarding her plans. Her expression became resigned.

'I thought all this was too good to be true. I know Pete is a bad man, and I've heard that he did wrong by you. He left me to come here and pack for the afternoon stage while he went to sort out his money affairs at the bank. Then he had to drop in on Hudson Brady to collect his recent earnings. You'll find him in one of those two places, unless he's in a saloon now, drinking away some of his dough.'

'Thanks, Madge. If Pete tells the law the truth about me then I won't kill him, although I've dreamed for years about putting him down in the dust for what he did.'

She shuddered, her hands going to her mouth, then she turned away from him and slumped down on the bed. Clayton eyed her for a moment, then turned swiftly and departed.

He left the boarding-house by the back door and stood for a moment on the back lots, looking around to get his bearings. He could see the back of the bank, but had no idea where Hudson Brady's office was situated. He decided that Bolam would have visited the bank first, so he could now be in Brady's office.

Reluctant to show himself on the street, Clayton figured that he had no other course if he wanted to pick up Bolam. Then he had second thoughts, for it came to him that if he caught Bolam he could not just confront Kline and insist on his innocence being proved. Bolam had only to say that he was under duress and the sheriff would turn him loose and try to throw Clayton himself in jail.

Thinking about it, Clayton realized that he had to find an alternative way of handling Bolam. If it had been just a matter of the robbery that had sent him to prison then he might have managed to convince Kline, but there was also the murder of Frank Butler that had been pinned on him. He knew Hondo Kline was a man of bull-headed temperament. From the outset he had believed Troy Clayton to be guilty, and nothing this side of hell could convince him otherwise.

Clayton drew his gun and checked its loads, his mind flitting over the broad face of his problem. Whatever his feelings, he had to take Bolam and drag him before the sheriff. If Bolam was sufficiently frightened then he would tell the truth. Clayton had always figured Pete for a coward.

He went into the nearest alley and made his way to the street end. Peering out of cover, he was surprised to see Pete Bolam coming along the sidewalk towards him, in the company of Slick Porter, the injured chief deputy sheriff.

It took Clayton a moment or two to recognize Bolam. The man had aged considerably over the past seven years. He was still the same small-boned, rat-faced, weasel-like man, but his face was plainly showing the dissolution of his past life. His dark eyes, deep-set in their fleshy sockets, were on the move all the time, darting furtive glances to all points of the compass as he constantly checked out his surroundings. His right hand did not stray far from the butt of the gun holstered on his hip. He seemed highly nervous, and there was a twitch in his left eye that was like perpetual motion.

Clayton stared at the man who had caused all his misfortunes, and, when

Troy thought that perhaps Bolam had also dry-gulched his father, a flame of desire for revenge burned bright in his breast. He drew his gun and waited, ready to put an end to his ceaseless hunt for Pete Bolam.

But Bolam and Porter turned abruptly and pushed through the batwings of a saloon. Clayton drew a deep breath and held it for a moment, fighting against the frustration boiling over inside him. He looked around the street. The town was still quiet. But he did not need to go near the saloon to check if it was busy. There were four horses belonging to members of the recently returned posse standing at the hitch-rail outside, and he had seen Hondo Kline himself entering the building only minutes before.

Clayton drew upon his last vestiges of patience and settled himself to wait for Bolam's reappearance. It had been so long now since he had first planned to grab Bolam and make him talk that it seemed to him it would never come about. But he fought down his emotions and waited stolidly.

After some minutes, four men emerged from the saloon, mounted their horses and rode along the street towards the livery barn. Clayton heaved a sigh. Time was not on his side. The longer he waited in the alley the more chance there was that someone would come along the street, recognize him, and raise the alarm.

Minutes later the batwings were thrust open again and Hondo Kline emerged to pause on the sidewalk and look around. The sheriff seemed even bigger than Clayton remembered, and was looking much older. His obesity seemed to have increased greatly in the last seven years, and when he moved off the sidewalk to cross the street he waddled rather than walked. Clayton watched him through slitted eyes, recalling the bad time the sheriff had given him upon the occasion of his arrest seven years earlier.

Clayton had always figured that Kline

was crooked although he had no evidence of that. When the sheriff disappeared into his office he drew a deep breath and continued to wait for a chance to get Bolam. But Kline emerged from his office immediately and looked around the street. Clayton faded back into the alley, and heard the bull-like roar of Kline's massive voice as the sheriff called for his chief deputy. The echoes of that penetrating voice trailed away across the town, and Porter emerged from the saloon in response and stood looking at the sheriff on the opposite side of the street.

'What in hell are you doing out of the office, Slick? Didn't I tell you to stand by all the time? I sure as hell didn't see you in the saloon. Was you hiding under a table?'

'You had your back to me,' Porter replied sullenly, and started across the street to the law office.

At that moment Bolam pushed through the batwings and stood watching the deputy's progress across the street. Clayton watched Bolam, silently praying that the man would come towards him, and a moment later Bolam turned to his left and came along the sidewalk towards the alley mouth, his stride sprightly and his narrow shoulders swinging.

Clayton checked the front of the law office. Kline had turned and re-entered the building and Porter was walking stolidly towards it. Bolam reached the alley and Clayton shot out a big hand, grasped Bolam's shoulder, and almost lifted the man bodily into the cover of the alley.

Bolam gasped in shock and instinctively reached for his holstered gun. But Clayton was ahead of him. He dragged Bolam's gun clear of leather and tossed it into the alley. Then he slammed the man against the nearest wall with enough force to drive the breath from his body. Bolam sagged, and Clayton held him upright with one hand.

'You don't know how I've longed for this moment, Pete,' Clayton said through his teeth.

'Troy Clayton!' Bolam stared at him through slitted eyes, his expression showing that his worst nightmare had come true. 'Where in hell did you spring from? They said you wouldn't dare show yourself in town.'

'I'd look for you in hell, Pete.'

'I ain't done nothing against you, Troy. You got the wrong man. It ain't me you want.'

'Convince me.'

Bolam opened his mouth to speak, then snapped it shut and compressed his lips. He stared at Clayton like an animal mesmerized by a snake.

'So you don't wanta talk. That's all right. Just answer the questions I want to ask you. First, why did you say in court that you saw me do the robbery? We both know you were lying.'

Bolam shook his head. He was trembling with fear. Clayton could feel him shaking. He tightened his grip on the smaller man and thrust him hard against the wall again, driving the breath from his body.

'I can't talk,' Bolam gasped. 'They'd kill me!'

'What makes you think I won't?' Clayton shook the man furiously. 'You better talk, Pete, and then mebbe I won't kill you. You were slated for hell the moment you lied in court and cost me seven years of my life. And you probably saddled me with a murder when I got out of jail. Who killed Frank Butler?'

'I don't know anything about that. I swear to God I don't.'

'Then let's talk about your lies in court. We both know you lied. You said you saw me do that robbery, Pete.'

'I was forced to say that! I would have been killed if I hadn't. They would have shot me down as I left the court. I did it to save my life, Troy. I didn't have a choice. They're ruthless men, and don't care who gets killed. What was a year in jail for you compared with the rest of my life for me?'

'Is that a fact? So tell me who put

you up to it and you might save your life now. I've dreamed of finding you and putting a slug through your lying face, Pete. That's what I'm gonna do if you don't spill the beans. And there's the matter of who dry-gulched my father. I reckon you know about that, don't you?'

'I swear to God, Troy. I didn't have anything to do with that.'

'I'm running out of patience, Pete. I got nothing to lose. If you don't tell the truth, I'll kill you. I guess you've heard how I turned killer when I got out of jail. I didn't have any choice. You set me on that trail, and every day since I've thought of what I'd do to you when I finally caught up with you.'

Bolam seemed to be paralysed with fear. His mouth opened and closed several times, like a fish out of water, and he made little moaning sounds as he tried to speak. Clayton shook him again.

'Who was behind it, Pete?' he insisted 'Someone paid you to lie about me.

Who? Was it Hudson Brady?'

'Brady?' Surprise replaced the fear in Bolam's eyes. 'You figure it was Brady?'

'I ain't figuring anything. I'm asking you. And you better come across with the truth. Lie to me now to get away and I'll hunt you down and kill you. If you've got any sense at all you'll start talking, you weasel!'

'It wasn't Brady. What made you pick him? Why would he wanta send a raw seventeen-year-old kid to jail?' He chuckled in a high-pitched tone. 'You spent all these years figuring it was Brady? Well, don't that beat all!'

'Cut it out, Pete. Open up. I want the truth, and I'll get it if I have to kill you.'

'Kill me and you'll never know who it was.' Bolam seemed to dredge up some resistance and a sneer came to his face. 'You can't kill me if you wanta know the truth, and that's a fact. And I ain't gonna tell you a thing, because you will kill me the minute I lay it on the line.'

'Don't count on that.' Clayton looked around the street. 'I just might cut my losses and finish you off, you snake.' He reached around to the back of Bolam's belt and drew a Bowie knife out of the sheath inside his pants. When he pressed the broad blade of the fearsome weapon against Bolam's cheek the man screeched in terror. 'If you wanta remain silent then I'll help you do it, Pete.' Clayton's tone was merciless. 'I've a mind to cut you loose from your tongue. You ruined my life with your lies, and I'll make you pay, one way or another.'

A footstep sounded nearby on the sidewalk and Clayton peered out of the alley to see Madge Austin coming towards him. She paused when she saw him. Her face was expressionless, but tension showed in her eyes. She came into the alley and gazed at Bolam, who was squirming in Clayton's grip.

'Is it true, Pete?' she demanded. 'Did your lies send this man to prison?'

Clayton shook Bolam. 'Tell her the truth,' he rasped.

'If it's true then everything is off

between us,' Madge continued. 'I wouldn't go away with a man who acted like that. I'm going back to the hotel right now to tell them I've changed my mind about leaving.'

'Clayton will kill me,' Bolam gasped. 'The minute I open my mouth he'll cut me to pieces. And if I did spill my guts, Troy, what could you do about it? Call the sheriff and make me tell him? Kline would say I confessed because I'm afraid of you. You don't have a chance. I knew seven years ago that you were a loser. You can't buck the play that's been set up. If you had any sense at all you'd get out fast, and never come back.'

'We're getting out together.' Clayton was aware that his time was running out. Every passing minute lessened his chances of remaining undetected. 'We'll talk later, when I'll have more time. You'd better go back to the hotel, Madge, and forget about this sidewinder. He ain't worth your attention.'

143

Madge looked contemptuously at Bolam, shaking her head. 'I really thought you were a good man, Pete,' she said. 'But what you are is showing in your face. You've saved me from making a fool of myself, Clayton. I hope you get what you want.'

She left the alley and went on along the sidewalk. Bolam made a sudden effort to free himself, throwing an ineffectual punch at Clayton who hit him hard on the jaw. Bolam dropped to his knees, shaking his head as his senses gyrated.

'You're making life tough for yourself, Pete,' Clayton said. 'I figured you had more sense. Come on, we're leaving town, and I'll make you talk if I have to roast you over a fire.'

He took hold of Bolam by the scruff of his neck and thrust him along the alley towards the back lots. Bolam protested vociferously and struggled violently, but was helpless in Clayton's grasp. They were passing the side door of the saloon when it was thrust open and two men appeared, embroiled in a fist fight. One of them sprawled backwards and collided with Bolam, who went down heavily.

Clayton palmed his gun, switching his knife to his left hand. Bolam scrambled to his feet, seemed about to take to his heels but saw Clayton's gun and halted. The man who had been knocked down rolled on to his back and lay gasping, his arms outflung. The man who had knocked him down looked at Clayton, saw the drawn gun, and lunged forward to grapple with him. Clayton tried to back off but came up against the opposite wall of the alley. The man blundered into him and Clayton tried to pull his gun hand clear but failed. The man's full weight thudded against him and his hair-triggered gun exploded raucously, filling the alley with thunder. The man fell away and dropped to the ground, a spreading patch of blood showing on his shirt front.

Clayton cursed as he grasped Bolam's

shoulder and set off at a run for the back lots. His ears were ringing from the crash of the shot. Bolam tried to pull away and Clayton cuffed him with the barrel of his gun. Bolam's legs gave way and he sprawled, but Clayton held him and dragged him along to the end of the alley.

Men were emerging from the side door of the saloon in response to the shot, and the next instant a gun crashed and a slug whined over Clayton's head. He stepped out of the alley and around the corner as more shooting erupted. Echoes growled away across the town. He risked a glance back into the alley, saw that several men were coming towards him in pursuit, and sent three shots into the alley, his muzzle canted to miss the men. The shooting sent the pursuers diving to the ground, and Clayton took a fresh grip on Bolam and ran with him towards the rear of the hotel.

Bolam was doing what he could to delay Clayton, and finally threw himself bodily to the ground and lay as dead, his face ashen, his hands shaking uncontrollably. Clayton threw a glance back at the alley. Men were emerging from it. He fired again, emptying his gun, but did not shoot to kill, and his shots had the desired affect. The men dived back into the alley.

'Bolam, I don't want you making a run for it now I've caught up with you.' Clayton looked around, wondering what to do for the best. He sheathed his knife and grabbed fresh shells from his cartridge-belt, thumbing them quickly into his smoking gun. 'I can't take you with me so I gotta make sure you stick around town for a spell.'

'No!' Bolam lifted his hands in terror. 'Don't shoot!'

'You never had any feelings for me.' Clayton pointed the big gun at Bolam's left shoulder and fired. The blast of the gun smashed out the silence. Bolam jumped convulsively when the slug bored through his flesh. then slumped into unconsciousness. Blood showed in a spreading stain at his shoulder.

Clayton ran for the rear of the hotel. Guns began to boom at his back, filling the air with crackling death. He hoped the Double B horse was still standing by the hotel, and a sigh of relief escaped him when he saw the animal. Grabbing up the reins, he swung into the saddle and spurred the animal into movement. The beast obeyed sluggishly, and Clayton realized that he was not going far. The horse was exhausted.

He twisted in the saddle and sent a couple of shots at the men now spreading out across the back lots. Five of them were intent on bringing him down, and he swerved the horse into an alley beside the bank and rode hell for leather towards the street. Bursting out of the alley, he hit the street at full gallop, gun held ready. His slitted gaze raked the street. The law office on the other side was just behind him as he turned to ride out of town. He glimpsed the obese figure of Hondo Kline appearing in the doorway, gun in hand, and Slick Porter was crowding the sheriff.

Spurring the tired horse, Clayton felt desperation begin to fill him. His back muscles were tensed in anticipation of the blasting impact of hot lead. He swung the horse to the left and entered an alley on Kline's side of the street, and the sheriff's eager shooting sent a stream of lead plunking harmlessly into the building on Clayton's right.

By the time he reached the back lots, Clayton could feel the horse faltering. He glanced around. There was no cover anywhere. He urged the horse to keep moving, but its pace was gone and it could barely manage a canter. Twisting in the saddle, he looked back, and saw Slick Porter emerging from the alley beside the jail. The chief deputy paused to raise a pistol and point it towards him.

Clayton fired two shots, aiming to miss, and Porter dived back into the cover of the alley. Then a shot crashed out from behind and the horse went down on its knees before cartwheeling into a heap on the hard ground. Clayton barely had time to kick his feet out of the stirrups. He dived sideways and hit the ground hard, rolling instantly, and finished up on his feet, his gun in his hand. He ran into the cover of the nearest alley.

His breath was rasping in his throat as he ran along the alley back towards the street, aware that he had to get clear of town in the next few minutes or he would be trapped. When he reached the street Troy peered around, then ducked back. A dozen men were moving around, drawn guns in their hands, all calling for news of the fugitive's whereabouts.

Clayton saw that he was standing in the cover of a ladies' dress shop, and realized that it belonged to Helen Vail, who was out at Tented C, nursing his father. The shop was locked, and he went back into the alley to the side door. There was no pursuit in the alley yet, and he put his shoulder to the door and smashed the lock. Entering, he holstered his gun and closed the door, thrusting the back of a chair under the handle, then leaned back and breathed deeply to recover his breath.

He had to get to the doctor's stable, collect his horse and head out of town. Pete Bolam wouldn't be going anywhere for a week or two. The shoulder wound would anchor the man in a spot where Clayton knew he would be able to get at him later. He reloaded his gun, and stiffened when he heard footsteps in the alley outside.

'He came into this alley,' a harsh voice rasped just outside the door, and Clayton cocked his gun.

'He wasn't planning on staying,' someone replied. 'We've got to get him before he leaves town.'

The men went on, and Clayton heard them at the alley mouth calling to the men back along the street. He went through to the front of the shop. A group of men was gathering outside, and he could hear their voices plainly as they discussed his whereabouts. Then they began to drift off in twos and threes, calling excitedly to each other to be careful in tackling him.

Clayton relaxed. He was safe for the moment, but had to get out of town. Although the afternoon was well advanced, darkness still lay several hours away, and he expected Sheriff Kline to have the whole town searched before nightfall.

7

Impatience gripped Clayton long before darkness came, and several times he got to his feet, gun in hand, when he heard voices outside the front door of the little shop. If discovered, he would sell his life dearly, and his finger trembled on the trigger of his deadly sixgun when the front door was tried by a rough hand.

'I reckon he's long gone,' a voice growled outside, barely a foot from where Clayton was standing on the inside. 'He knows Kline will have him shot on sight. He ain't stupid. He's been on the run for seven years.'

'He didn't get the chance to make it to town limits,' someone replied. 'I figure he's holed up, waiting for darkness. Then he'll make a run for it.'

The two men moved on. Clayton could hear the sound of their receding footsteps on the boardwalk. Shadows were filling the little shop. He stretched his cramped limbs, aware that he would have to move fast when it was time to go because the town was still aroused. They expected him to stir soon, and would be ready for him.

He peered through a window, and curbed his impatience when he discovered that he could still see the buildings on the opposite side of the wide street. He judged that it would be another hour before he could think of leaving. His stomach was complaining that it was empty, and he was parched. He looked around in the room at the rear of the shop, hoping to find something to eat, or at least some water to drink, but there was nothing. He smiled mirthlessly, thinking that every man's hand was against him. He did not have a single friend in the world. Then he thought of Barney Draper and readjusted his thoughts.

When full darkness finally came he went to the side door and let himself out. Holding his gun in his right hand, he moved slowly through the darkness to the back lots. He needed to get his horse from the doctor's barn, but he did not make the mistake of walking through the town. He guessed that Kline would have his men out for at least another couple of hours.

He crossed the back lots, walking away from the town, and when he was clear of the buildings he started to circle at a distance from the buildings. When he reached the trail leading into town he was a hundred yards out from the town limit. He crossed the trail and made his way back to the rear of the doctor's house.

Now the darkness was impenetrable. The doctor's house was invisible in the night. Clayton dropped flat by the barn and lay motionless while he listened for movement. It was possible that his horse had been discovered in the barn, and if so there would be a reception committee waiting for him. He lay as dead for twenty minutes, fighting his impatience, and finally decided that he was alone.

He passed the barn and went to the back door of the doctor's house. Amos would expect him to call in before leaving, and when he tried the back door he found it unbolted and slipped into the dark interior. There was a strip of light showing under the door leading to the front of the house and Clayton moved stealthily towards it. His gun was in his hand when he silently opened the door, and a sigh of relief escaped him when he looked into the room and saw the doctor and his wife relaxing inside.

Amos got to his feet when he saw Clayton, and there was a grim smile on his lined face.

'I've been worried about you, Troy,' he observed. 'When I heard all the shooting earlier. I feared the worst. But there were only two wounded men out there, and Bolam was one of them.'

'You've got Bolam?' Clayton nodded. 'I had to shoot him. I need him to stay in one place to get to him when I want.'

'You certainly managed that. Bolam will be on his back for a couple of weeks. I've got him in my sick room with Barney. But Hudson Brady was here a short time ago. He wants Bolam taken out to Double B soon as he can be moved.'

'Is that a fact?' Clayton frowned. 'Why would Brady be concerned about a two-bit gunnie like Bolam?'

'Bolam has been Brady's odd-job man for years. He's taken care of the little problems Brady's had from time to time.'

'Like framing me with a robbery, then a murder!' Clayton pinched his lips together, his eyes narrowed as he tried to make sense of his past. He shook his head. It was all beyond him. 'I'd better get moving, Doc. Thanks for your help.'

'I happen to believe in your innocence, Troy. Your horse is ready-saddled in the barn. I was out there a short time ago and I don't think Kline has got anyone watching the place. I figure I'm above suspicion around here. Get clear and keep on the move.'

'How is Barney?'

'Don't worry about him. He's safe here. I'll come with you to the barn, just in case.'

'No. Don't do that. If anyone is watching, and there's shooting, you could get caught in the crossfire. I'll just fade away and all the excitement will die down.'

'Before you go you'd better have something to eat.' Mrs Amos got to her feet and went to the door. 'I'm keeping a meal hot for you, Troy, and I've sacked up some supplies. I guess you can't go to the store like an ordinary man. Come and sit down at the kitchen table. You must eat regularly.'

'Thanks.' Clayton was touched by her kindness. He followed her into the kitchen, and the smell of cooked food made him aware of his hunger. He ate ravenously when the meal was placed before him, and drank two cups of the coffee Mrs Amos poured for him. But he was impatient to be on the move, and arose from the table immediately he had eaten the meal.

'I've got to get moving,' He hitched up his gunbelt. 'I'll never be able to thank you enough for helping me out.' He took the provisions and departed. Amos fetched the black gelding out of the stable while Clayton remained in the background.

'Good luck, Troy,' the old medic said. 'I don't know where all this will end, but I hope you're one of those still standing when the gunsmoke clears. I know you won't take my advice and ride out. You're gonna push this now to the bitter end, and I can't say that I blame you. It was on the cards that some day you would come back, and I must admit there is a strong smell of crookedness in the air around here.'

'I wish you could tell me more about that,' Clayton responded. 'I sure as hell don't have the faintest idea what is going on.'

'I get around a lot in my business, and hear rumours that begin to add up after a time. But I don't have a notion who's back of it all. A man can't act on suspicion alone, Troy. But I've got Pete Bolam in my care now, and mebbe I can wheedle something out of him before Brady takes him off to Double B. If I do learn anything, how can I get word to you?'

'I'll drop in on you from time to time, Doc. You can bet that I won't be far away. It was in this town that my downfall was planned, and I reckon it'll be around here that the truth will come out. So long, Doc.'

Clayton grasped his reins and walked off into the night, leading his horse. He moved out slowly across the back lots, and when he was alone in the darkness he paused and looked back at the lights of the town, aware that his frustration was strong inside him.

A sigh escaped him. He had figured it would be easy to prove his innocence. All he had to do was drop on to Pete

Bolam and scare the truth out of the man. But it hadn't turned out like that. Bolam had proved to be tougher than expected, and Clayton knew now that he would not be able to scare the truth out of him. So who else around town might know about what had happened seven years before?

Hondo Kline! A picture of the sheriff arose in Clayton's mind and he nodded slowly. He had always suspected that Kline was mixed up in local crookedness. He could remember when he had spent time in the town jail, before being sent to prison. Kline had certainly acted like a man who gave his ambitions priority over his duty. In particular, he remembered an incident in the law office in which Kline had received a bulging envelope from Pete Bolam. The sheriff had looked round, caught the eye of the youthful Troy Clayton, locked in the big cage at the rear of the office, and grinned knowingly as he stuffed the envelope into a pants' pocket.

Clayton's teeth clicked together at the memory. So Hondo Kline had been on the take in those days! And Pete Bolam had always worked for Hudson Brady.

So Brady had been paying Kline for services rendered, and the only worthwhile action taking place around town at that time had been the robbery allegedly committed by the wild-blooded, hotheaded Troy Clayton.

Clayton squared his shoulders. Some of it was coming back to him now. Seven years on the run from the law had dulled his memory, and details of some of his suspicions had faded under the pressures of staying free of the law. But he figured that Hondo Kline had a lot to answer for, and he turned resolutely to retrace his circuitous route around the town. He reached the rear of the jail and tethered his horse in a thicket a hundred yards out from the buildings.

Walking in across the rough ground behind the jail, Clayton steeled himself to do what was necessary. He had to get to Kline and throw a scare into the big sheriff. Kline was a bully, and might just cave in under threat of death. A tense smile touched Clayton's thin lips. If there was a flaw in the sheriff's character then he would find it.

He entered the alley beside the jail and edged his way forward to a lighted window just inside the front end of the alley. Peering through the window, he saw the whole of the front office, and his eyes glinted at the sight of Kline seated behind his desk. Slick Porter was standing by the door, apparently on the point of leaving.

Kline was talking at great length and Porter was nodding his head. But Clayton could not hear what was being said. The chief deputy opened the door, but paused because the sheriff was still in full flow. Then Kline waved a hand and Porter departed and closed the door.

Clayton remained to one side of the window, out of the light issuing from it.

He gazed hungrily at the sheriff, longing to get to grips with him. Kline had figured largely on Clayton's list of men to confront, but had always been second to Pete Bolam. Now that Bolam was safe for the moment it was Kline's turn to face his moment of truth. The big lawman had a lot to answer for, and Clayton was impatient to ask the questions that might bring enough information to clear up the mystery surrounding him.

But he controlled his impatience and waited stolidly, wondering how best to approach Kline. During the fifteen minutes in which he watched the lawman no fewer than four men entered the office, no doubt to report on the search that was being made for Troy Clayton. It would be impossible to confront Kline in the office, and Clayton forced himself to remain in cover and await developments.

Thirty minutes later, Slick Porter re-entered the office. Kline immediately got to his feet, stuck his hat on his head and waddled towards the door. Porter took the sheriff's place on the chair behind the desk, and, as Kline left the office, Clayton moved to the alley mouth and watched the sheriff's massive figure, like a mountain lion stalking its prey.

Kline ambled across the street and went into a saloon. Clayton moved back into the cover of the alley mouth and waited, watching the batwings of the saloon. It didn't matter to him how long it took. He was going to confront Kline.

Several more men arrived at the law office and entered to report to Porter. None stayed more than a few moments, and when two of them arrived and left together, Clayton heard one of them complain to the other that they had been wasting their time looking for Troy Clayton. It was obvious that the gunman had departed for other pastures. The two men went into the saloon, and the watching Clayton assumed that the hunt for him inside town limits was finally being scaled down.

An hour passed before Hondo Kline emerged from the saloon, and Clayton listened to the lawman's booming voice as the sheriff went along the sidewalk, talking to various passers-by. Clayton followed carefully, remaining on the opposite side of the street, watching the sheriff's massive figure as it passed several street lamps.

Kline entered another saloon, and Clayton sighed, impatient now to confront the lawman. A plan was forming in the back of his mind that just might jolt Kline into admitting complicity in the plot that had sent a youth to jail seven years before. The more he thought about it the better he liked it, and, when Kline appeared on the street once more, Clayton was raring to go.

He knew that seven years ago Kline had regularly slept in his jail, using a bed in an empty cell. The lawman owned a shack near the far end of town but rarely used it. Now the big star-toter waddled along the sidewalk and continued past the law office, moving swiftly for a man of his immense proportions. Clayton followed at a distance, and relief filled him when Kline entered a shack on the outskirts of town.

Moving in, Clayton was only feet from the door when Kline lit a lamp inside the shack. When the sheriff turned to close the door, Clayton confronted him, gun in hand, the muzzle pointing steadily at Kline's wide expanse of shirt front. Kline froze and stared at Clayton as if seeing a ghost. His mouth dropped open but no sound issued from it.

Clayton went forward and Kline gave way, his hands lifting shoulder high. Clayton entered the shack and closed the door. He studied the quaking sheriff for long moments, and had to struggle against an instinctive desire to plant a bullet in Kline's guts.

'You can't be surprised to see me,

Kline,' Clayton grinned. 'Surely you expected me to come after you, the way you let me take the blame for that robbery.'

'You're making a big mistake, staying around town.' Kline's voice was deep-toned, and rumbled out of the depths of his barrel chest. He was a massively built man, tall as well as obese. His face was like a full moon, broad in the forehead and fleshy, with high cheek-bones and a massive, square chin. Piggish eyes were almost lost in the wrinkled flesh surrounding their sockets. But now his habitual bluster was gone and fear gripped him, showing in his manner and the slitted eyes that stared at Clayton in disbelief.

'You're the one who made a mistake, Kline. You should have had me killed seven years ago instead of sending me to prison. I spoke to Pete Bolam this afternoon before I had to shoot him, and he told me everything that went on seven years ago.'

'He did?' A narrowing of the eyes

warned Clayton that Kline's devious mind was beginning to work. 'Then you better tell me what he said. He'd lie to save his own skin. He sent you to jail in the first place. Me, I was only doing my duty as I saw it. There was evidence that you committed the robbery, and I put you where you belonged.'

'Get rid of your gun-belt before we go any further.' Clayton motioned with his pistol and Kline unbuckled the belt, allowing it to fall to the floor. 'Step back from it and sit down in that chair over by the stove.'

Clayton pushed home the bolt on the inside of the door, effectively barring it, and moved to sit on a corner of the small table while Kline dropped his massive weight into a solid wooden chair that creaked and groaned in protest.

'The pigeons are coming home to roost, Kline. You've had a good run. Bolam told me you let him handle that lie about me doing the robbery. I even saw him hand you a package of dough while I was behind bars in your jail. You're in Brady's pocket. You've had a rake-off from every dirty deal you closed your eyes to.'

'Pete told you all that, did he?' Kline moistened his lips. 'I allus figured he had a good line in lies. What else did you think he'd do if you had a gun on him? Bolam would railroad his mother to get himself off the hook.'

'He told me about the way I was framed for Frank Butler's murder.' Clayton was trying shots in the dark, and grinned when he saw Kline's fleshy face turn pale. 'Someone should hang for that, but it ain't gonna be me now. I got Bolam laid low with a bad shoulder wound, and when I need him he's gonna stand up and tell the whole town just what's been going on around here.'

'Bolam is lying through his teeth. He figured to get you off his back, and he's dumped you in my lap. Well that won't help you or him at all. I got a lot on Bolam, and after this I'll see that he gets what's coming to him.' Kline leaned back in his chair and grinned. 'What you figure to do now? You thought you was so allfired clever coming in here. But you ain't got a thing that will clear you of the mud we stuck on you.'

Clayton cocked his gun and moved forward until the black muzzle jabbed the sheriff between the eyes.

'You're looking hell between the eyes, Kline,' he grated. 'To tell you the truth I don't care much what I have to do. I'd as soon cut my losses, kill everyone lined up against me, then light out for other parts. But there's something I want to get the truth on. Who dry-gulched my father? And why? Someone's got to pay for that.'

'Didn't Pete tell you about it?' Kline grinned. 'You won't kill me, Troy. You need me alive, and whatever is said in here, I wouldn't repeat it in front of witnesses. You ain't got a leg to stand on. You're wanted by the law and no one, but no one, is gonna pay heed to what you say. You're a loser, and the best advice I can give you is get out of town and keep going.'

Clayton was infuriated by Kline's resistance, aware that the sheriff was correct in his summing up of the situation. He could make these men talk only under fear of death, but they knew he could not kill them because their knowledge would die with them. He cocked his gun and placed the muzzle over the tip of the sheriff's fleshy nose, putting pressure on it and forcing Kline's head back on its thick neck.

'If I can't get anything out of you then I might as well cut my losses,' he grated. 'You're facing it right now, Kline. I'm desperate enough to kill you and be sorry for it afterwards.'

Sweat broke out on the sheriff's fleshy face. The chair creaked ominously as he leaned back away from the prodding gun muzzle. His fleshy lips moved soundlessly, and real fear showed in his coarse features.

'How will it help you if I do admit to

some of what you say?' he gasped. 'You couldn't go into court and tell the judge about it. You'd never make it. The men in town are roused up about you. They'll shoot you on sight.'

'Write down on paper exactly what happened, in the form of a confession, and I'll take my chances with it.' Clayton cocked his gun and the metallic clicks sounded loud in the tense silence.

A shudder ran through Kline's heavy frame and he moistened his lips. His eyes closed and he slumped in the chair. For a moment Clayton figured that the crooked lawman had passed out, but Kline opened his eyes and nodded.

'If it'll please you I'll write down anything you want,' he said hoarsely. 'There's pen, ink and writing paper in that cupboard over there.'

'Get them and sit at the table. Don't try anything, Kline, or you'll finish up in hell quicker than you can blink. The time for playing games is over. Get down to it, and quick.'

He moved back and Kline heaved himself to his feet. He went to the cupboard and took out pen, ink and paper. Sitting at the table, he looked up at Clayton, and the cunning expression was back in his eyes.

'You better tell me what you want me to write,' he said, dipping the pen in the ink.

'You know what to write. Put it down as it happened. And don't think you're out of the wood yet. I've got a big score to settle around here.'

Kline looked at him for a few moments, then started to write, and Clayton stood watching the crooked lawman intently. Kline wrote for some minutes, his fleshy lips pursed, his head tilted to one side as he concentrated on what he was doing. He finally threw down the pen and slumped back in his seat. Looking up at Clayton, he shook his head.

'It's all down there,' he said. 'Everything you want to hear. Bolam did it all, and framed you with it. He shot your father three weeks ago. I didn't do anything to stop him because he works for Brady, and nobody can go against Brady and live. But you ain't gonna be able to do anything with that statement, Clayton. I only got to stand up in court and say I wrote it while you had a gun on me and it won't be worth a plugged nickel.'

'I'll take my chance with it.' Clayton picked up the sheet of paper and read it through. He was surprised that the sheriff had written the truth, and waved the paper around to dry the ink. 'I figure you're the one who should get out of town fast, before this gets out,' he said. 'Folks will be able to put two and two together, Kline, and, even if this statement won't stand up in court, you can't fool the townsfolk any more. Some of them will suspect what's been going on, and I reckon it finishes you around here.'

'Don't kid yourself.' Kline's harsh voice sounded even more hoarse than usual. 'All I've given you is the deadwood on Bolam, and if you hope to rely on him as a witness then you're a bigger fool than I thought. You better up stakes before you get in any deeper. When Brady gets wind of this he'll have Bolam killed quicker than you can blink.'

Clayton tightened his grip on his pistol and swung the weapon in a tight arc, crashing the barrel against the side of Kline's big head. The sheriff uttered a cry of shock and slid sideways off his seat. He landed on the floor with a crash that jarred the shack, and lay on his back with his arms outflung, breathing stentorously through his gaping mouth.

Clayton gazed down at the inert lawman for some moments, his thoughts fast moving. Then he extinguished the lamp and moved to the door. The darkness was impenetrable, and he fumbled with the bolt before the door opened. He paused in the doorway to fold the statement Kline had written, and pushed the document into a breast pocket.

Stepping out into the night, he paused to look around, and a harsh voice yelled at him from the dense shadows out front. At the same instant a gun blasted, its reddish muzzle flame shattering the close darkness. Clayton heard the thud of a bullet striking the door a scant inch from his right ear, and his gun was cocked and ready for action as he instinctively threw himself to the left and hit the ground hard on his shoulder.

He rolled away from the doorway as a fusillade of shots erupted from several points nearby, ripping the night with flame and noise. Voices were yelling, punctuating the raucous thunder of the guns. Clayton kept moving, and barely managed to stay one step ahead of the flailing death that struck at him . . .

8

Clayton's ears were battered by the noise of shots as he rolled and squirmed his way to the left-hand corner of the shack. He dived around the corner, his progress marked by bullets tearing into the woodwork about him. Getting to his feet, he sprinted along the alley towards the back lots, and managed to turn a rear corner before more slugs came streaking after him.

He paused to get his breath, and risked a look into the alley. Two guns were firing blindly at him into the darkness, and he ducked as a bullet crackled past his head. He ran across the back lots, making for the spot where he had left his horse. Behind him the shooting petered out, and as the echoes of gunfire faded he heard voices yelling excitedly.

He reached the spot where the gelding was waiting, and the animal whinnied softly when he approached. A sigh of relief escaped him as he swung into the saddle. He sat in the darkness, listening for signs of pursuit, but nothing stirred or sounded now. He wheeled the horse and rode out slowly, not wanting the sound of hoofs to carry in the night.

When he was well clear of town, Clayton reined in and considered his next move. Kline had said Brady would have Bolam killed the instant he learned that the man had confessed about the frame-up seven years ago. So Bolam had to be protected. Clayton sighed and went on slowly. He crossed the trail, circled to the other side of town, and edged his way towards the rear of the doctor's house. He left his horse in cover away from the medico's barn in case he had to leave in a hurry.

His eyes were accustomed to the darkness, and he walked silently to the rear of the house. The back door was bolted, and he walked around the building to the street. The lights of the town were like yellow pools in the darkness along the whole length of the main street, and towards the centre of town there were figures moving around, silhouetted against the lamps.

A rider came along the street and galloped out of town. Voices sounded as another search got under way, and Clayton remained in the shadows at a corner of the house to check the progress of those pitched against him. He stiffened when a shadow moved towards the house, and his gun was in his hand as he stepped forward to confront the figure.

'Is that you, Doc?' he whispered, and cocked his gun.

'Troy?' Frank Amos approached him slowly. 'I thought you'd be long gone by now. You've really stirred up the town. I heard the shooting and went to check on the dead and wounded, but no one was hurt except Kline and he only got a lump on his head. He's roused out every able-bodied man to hunt for you. When I left him he was talking about a house-to-house search.'

'I need to speak to Bolam, Doc. I got a statement from Kline which ain't worth the paper it's written on. But if Bolam sees it he'll figure Kline has blown the whistle on him and might decide to cut his losses. If he talks about what really happened, and figures that his life is on the line, then he'll make a good witness to have. But I'll have to get him away from here or Brady will have him killed.'

'Do you figure Brady is back of the crookedness?' Amos glanced over his shoulder. Voices were sounding quite close and coming closer. 'They're beginning to search the town. You better fade into the shadows and wait until they've passed, Troy. Then we'll go inside.'

Clayton stepped back around the corner and waited, gun in hand. His thoughts raced as he tried to plan a course of action. He heard the doctor challenge two men who arrived, and listened to the short conversation that took place. The men wanted to search the house, and Amos took them inside. Clayton waited impatiently. Time seemed to drag, but eventually the men emerged from the house, thanking the doctor profusely before departing to continue their search.

'It's all right now, Troy,' Amos said when the two men had entered the house next door. 'Come on in.'

Clayton holstered his gun and followed the doctor into the house. Amos led the way to his sick room, and Clayton paused in the doorway to look at Barney Draper and Pete Bolam, who were lying in adjacent beds. Barney was awake, reading a newspaper, but Bolam seemed to be asleep.

'Hi, Barney, how are you doing?' Clayton went to the side of Draper's bed.

'Troy! Am I glad to see you!' Draper's weathered face was pale but he didn't seem to be in any pain. 'I wanta get out of here. I can't stand the smell of this skunk.' He threw a glance at Bolam, who had opened his eyes at the sound of voices. 'You sure been raising hell around town, huh? I been hearing shooting on and off all afternoon. I'm sure glad you put a lead pill into Bolam, and it's a pity you didn't kill him.'

Clayton took Kline's statement from his pocket and handed it to Amos, who read it, then looked up questioningly.

'This won't hold up in a court,' he said.

'I'm aware of that. But it will show Bolam exactly where he stands, and that any statement he makes of his own free will, and in front of witnesses, will hold water. Read it out aloud, Doc. I guess Pete will wanta know how he's fixed around here.'

Amos read Kline's scribbled words. Clayton watched Bolam's face, and saw a host of expressions flit across the sharp features. When the doctor had finished, Bolam shook his head.

'You're trying to run a sandy on me, Clayton,' he rasped. 'Kline would never put anything down in writing.'

'Don't fool yourself, Pete. I put the fear of God into Kline and he came up with this. You and I know it's the truth, and there are some details written here that I didn't know about. But you know they could only have come from Kline. You're the fall guy in this, Pete. Kline said Brady will have you killed the minute he learns you've put the finger on him. And two of Kline's men were in here checking that I wasn't around. They saw you, and will report to Kline. So you're gonna have to rely on me to keep you alive. That's a twist, huh? For years I wanted to see you dead. Now I've got to save you.'

'You can't get round me like that.' Bolam shook his head. 'I got nothing to say.'

'Whether you talk or not, I've got to keep you in one piece. Brady will have a couple of men here before morning. Is Bolam able to travel, Doc?'

184

'If his life is in danger then you'll have to take him,' Amos decided. 'But he couldn't sit a horse. That slug you put into him struck a bit low. If he gets shaken up he could bleed to death.'

'I thought of taking him and Barney out to Tented C, but maybe that's too far. Is there somewhere they would be safe around town?'

'What about my shack?' Barney demanded.

'That'll be the first place Kline will search.' Clayton shook his head. He looked at Amos.

The doctor was frowning. 'I can't help you there, Troy,' he said. 'I don't think you can trust anyone in town. There's no telling who's working with Brady. I didn't think Hondo Kline could sink so low, but if Brady's got him in his back pocket then who else is involved?' He shrugged and shook his head. 'I don't know what to think any more.'

'I ain't going out to Tented C,' Bolam groaned as he tried to drag himself up

185

in the bed. There was a bloodstain on the thick bandaging on his injured shoulder.

'What you got against the spread?' Barney demanded.

'I don't want to go out there.' Bolam compressed his lips. There was a dogged expression on his sharp features.

'We've got to think of something, and fast. There's a real chance that a couple of gunnies will come sneaking in here before dawn to put out your light, Pete.' Clayton rubbed his chin. Then he nodded. 'I've got it. Helen is out at Tented C, nursing my father. I hid out in her shop earlier, and got away with it. Barney and Bolam can stay there. The living quarters over the shop will be big enough for them. What do you think, Doc?'

'It's probably the only chance you've got,' Amos agreed. 'I don't want Bolam here any longer than he has to be. If a couple of Brady's men do show up then innocent people might get hurt. He should be all right making a short move. I'll give you a hand to get him across to the shop, but we'd better wait until after the town has been searched.'

Clayton agreed. Barney was grinning, happy to be useful again. Bolam's face, with its grim expression, revealed exactly what he was thinking. He looked like a man who could feel a rope around his neck.

'Gimme a gun, Troy,' Barney begged. 'You'll need someone to keep an eye on Bolam, and I volunteer for the job.'

'You won't need a gun on him,' Amos said. 'Pete won't trouble anyone for a couple of weeks.'

Clayton sat down on the side of Bolam's bed. He gazed at the gun-man with slitted eyes. Bolam moved uneasily.

'Kline said you dry-gulched my father, Pete,' Clayton observed.

'Not me. What for would I wanta do that?'

'Why did you set out to frame me seven years ago?' Clayton shook his head. 'I figure you shot my father for the same reason. Is someone hoping to take over Tented C?'

'That don't seem right,' Barney cut in. 'If someone was planning to move in they would have made their second move long before this.'

'I agree.' Clayton nodded. 'But Pete knows the reason and I just want him to think about it for a spell. When he accepts that I'm about to try and save his life he might have a change of heart and come up with some of the answers I need. Understand this, Pete. Whatever I do is with the intention of getting at the truth, and I wouldn't hesitate to drop you if I found a better source. I had Kline shaking in his boots. He seems to know as much about the past as you, and I reckon if I see him again he'll crack wide open and start spilling his guts.'

Bolam's face looked as if it had been carved out of stone. There was a hunted expression in his eyes. He shook his head slowly, as if denying the truth of

Clayton's words, but his manner suggested that he mentally agreed, and Clayton experienced a spark of hope that at last he might be making progress.

'Will you let me take Kline's statement to Bill Coppard, the lawyer?' Amos asked. 'I'd like to get his opinion on it. I doubt if it would stand up in a court, but it might be enough to get the mayor and the town council questioning Kline's right to continue as the sheriff. We just might be able to crack open the conspiracy that's been formed around here.'

'Sure.' Clayton nodded. 'The more honest men who see it the easier it will be for me to convince folks of my innocence.'

'And if these honest men get their hands on Bolam they'll soon make him talk,' Barney opined. 'I'm looking forward to the next few days. A lot of two-bit crooks around here will get their comeuppance, and some of them will hang when the truth finally comes out. Don't forget that Frank Butler was murdered, and if Troy didn't do it then who did?' He eyed Bolam for a moment, and the man seemed to squirm. 'You sure got a bad conscience, Pete,' he observed. 'I reckon you're one of the guilty men we'll have to take care of when the time comes.'

Clayton handed Kline's statement to the doctor, who folded it carefully and put it into a breast pocket. Amos smiled encouragingly and patted the pocket.

'Don't look so worried, Troy,' he said. 'I'm going to take a walk around town to see what's going on. I'll come back when the search is completed, and we'll move Bolam out.' He paused to consider, frowning, and then seemed to reach a decision. 'I wonder if it wouldn't be better to take the bull by the horns and go for what you want, Troy.'

'How do you mean?' Clayton was immediately interested.

'I'm due to play poker tonight with a small circle of close friends.' Amos nodded. 'We play every Friday evening, and have done so for years. Leo Wade, the mayor, Matthew Wilson, the banker, and Bill Coppard, the lawyer. We're playing at Wade's house tonight, and it might be a good idea to have you accompany me. With Kline's statement, and Bolam to back you up, we might be able to swing the scales in your favour.'

'I ain't saying nothing to no one,' Bolam rasped.

'I think you know when to take your chance.' Amos spread his hands. 'You're trapped right in the middle of this, Bolam, and there's only one way out for you. I can see it clearly, but at the moment you can't. So think about it and you should see sense. Barney, I'll bring you a gun, and if you want to help Troy then you'll make sure nothing bad happens to Bolam.'

'You can bet on it,' Barney replied cheerfully.

'I'll go with you, Doc,' Clayton said. 'I've got nothing to lose. But how will these friends of yours react when they learn that I'm Troy Clayton?'

'I'll vouch for you, and that will go a long way with them. Let's go now. I'll fetch you a gun, Barney.'

Clayton grimaced as he followed the doctor down to his treatment room. Amos took a sixgun out of a drawer, checked it, and went back to the sick room. Clayton forced himself to remain patient until Amos returned.

'You'd better stay a couple of paces behind me when we go along the street,' the doctor said as they left the house. 'Fortunately, Wade's home is at this end of the town. Do you remember Wade? He owned the lumber yard around the time you had your troubles.'

'The name sounds familiar, but it's been seven years.' Clayton shrugged. 'But I'll bet he knows who I am.'

'There was never any love lost between Wade and Brady. But that's how it is with everyone who ever had a business in this town. Brady has been crowding out the competition for years.'

Clayton walked in the doctor's shadow and they went away from the town centre. Eventually they turned in at the gateway of a large, two-storey house. A lamp was burning at the front door, and there was a tall figure standing before it, waiting to be admitted. Clayton tensed, dropping a hand to the butt of his holstered gun, but Amos greeted the man pleasantly.

'Evening, Matt. All set to continue that winning run you started last week?'

'Evening, Frank. It made a change to be in the chips.'

'Do you remember Matt Wilson, Troy? He's run the bank in town ever since there was a bank. Matt, this is Troy Clayton.'

'Troy Clayton? Henry Clayton's youngest son! He's the man Kline is searching the town for.'

'The one and the same.'

The door was opened then, and Clayton recognized Leo Wade as the man greeted his friends. Wade, the town mayor, was in his fifties, prosperous-looking and well dressed. He stared at Clayton, and frowned when he recognized him.

'That's Troy Clayton, Frank,' he observed. 'Heck, the whole town is roused up about him. What's he doing here?'

'We need to put a problem to Bill. Has he arrived yet?'

'Been here for the last twenty minutes, and impatient to start playing. Come in. The house has already been searched so I doubt we shall be bothered by Kline's men again.'

Clayton felt as if he were walking into a trap when he entered the house. He removed his hat and stood stiffly by the door. Wade led the way into an inner room, and Bill Coppard, seated at a table already prepared for playing poker, looked up and smilingly greeted his friends. Then his face sobered and he peered intently at Clayton. Getting to his feet, he came forward quickly, looking at Clayton as if he could not believe his eyes.

'Yes, Bill, it is Troy Clayton.' Amos seemed to be enjoying the shock he was causing.

'You've been rousing up the town most of the day,' the lawyer observed. 'All that shooting. Did you take part in that?'

'Only a few shots,' Clayton admitted. 'I dropped on to Pete Bolam this afternoon and wanted him to stay in one place for a spell so I put a slug through his shoulder.'

'Bolam is resting up in my sick room at the moment,' Amos said. He reached into his breast pocket and produced the statement Hondo Kline had written. 'Look at this, Bill.'

'You're up to something, Frank.' Coppard scanned the statement, then whistled silently. 'I suppose you forced Kline to write this, huh?' he demanded. Respect showed in his eyes.

'I persuaded him,' Clayton amended.

'Then it won't hold up in a court of

law.' Coppard shook his head. 'That's a great pity.'

Wade held out his hand and the lawyer passed the statement to him. Wade read it in silence, and when he looked up at Clayton there was a grin on his weathered face.

'Kline actually wrote and signed this?' he demanded. 'You must have thrown a helluva scare into him.'

'It's all his own work,' Clayton nodded.

'That's what a reputation does for you.' Wade was smiling. 'Of course it won't do for the court, but it gives us a lever to use against Kline. He's admitted to rigging evidence, states that he knows Bolam is guilty of killing Frank Butler, and admits to taking back-handers from Hudson Brady. We can make him resign on the strength of this. Where is Pete Bolam?'

'In my sick room.' Amos glanced at Clayton and winked. 'Don't worry about Bolam. He's feeling very sorry for himself at the moment, and if Brady sends men to kill him, and they failed, he'll get the message that it will be better to co-operate with us. Once he starts talking there'll be no stopping him.'

'Can you protect Bolam from Brady?' Coppard asked. 'He's the ace in the hole.'

'Troy can do it, if anyone can,' Amos smiled.

'I don't understand any of this.' Clayton shook his head. 'Everyone in town is against me, but you're talking as if I've done you a big favour.'

'The only men against you are those who run with Kline or collect wages from Brady,' Wade said. 'Those two have had a stranglehold on Sunset Ridge for more years than I care to remember. Every crime that has been committed around here was done on Brady's orders. I'm thinking there are more riff-raff than honest men in town, so it's a good thing you've come back to us, Troy. We need someone like you — talented with a gun, and with a reputation to back your play.'

'Me?' Clayton shook his head. 'I'm wanted by the law. I've been blamed for Frank Butler's murder.'

Wade shook his head. He looked at Coppard. 'You acted as the coroner at Butler's inquest, didn't you, Bill?'

'I surely did. There was no evidence that pointed to you being the killer, Troy.'

'A knife with my initials on it was found,' Clayton persisted.

'True. But there was no evidence to link it with Troy Clayton.' Coppard shrugged. 'If I remember correctly, there was a Tom Carver and a Thad Collins around town at the time of the murder. Either man could have owned that knife, and both worked for Brady. Kline carried out an extensive investigation and found no proof against anyone. He started the rumour that it must have been your knife because you had been recently freed from prison and were the most likely candidate for murder.'

'So I'm not wanted here by the law?' Clayton's eyes were filled with disbelief.

'Not unless you've committed crimes anywhere in Texas,' Coppard replied. 'We've all heard of your reputation, but, like all reputations, much of it is based on hearsay. There has not been one scrap of proof that you ever stole or murdered.'

'I was sent to jail for robbery,' Clayton said bitterly.

'On the evidence of a man of dubious character,' Amos pointed out. 'But Bolam may now retract his statement, which would clear you.'

'And we can hire you to do a job around town which would suit your particular talents.' Wade looked at each of the other men in turn, and all nodded, their expressions taut with determination. 'We need a fast gun to wear the town marshal's badge. I'm offering it to you, Troy, with our full support. Take it and set to work cleaning out the bad men who have gathered in our midst. We have got to fight fire with fire.'

'You came home because of your father,' Amos observed, 'and evil men had the whole county on the look-out for you, ready to shoot you on sight. You've got a lot of scores to settle, Troy, and I think this is the best way you can do it.'

'I'll go along with that,' Coppard said. 'Take the badge and do what you're good at. You need to take on these bad men and beat them at their own game, and the marshal's badge will give more power to your gun.'

Clayton remained silent for some moments, thinking over the situation. Then he nodded slowly.

'I'll take the badge,' he said. 'And I'll try to do the job you want. I'll arrest all those who have been playing this community for suckers, and if I kill anyone it will be in defence of my own life.'

'That sounds fine to me.' Wade reached into a vest pocket and he produced a law star with MARSHAL etched into it. 'I put this in my pocket the moment I heard you were back. Pin it on, Troy, and I'll swear you in. Then you'll be all set to go.'

Clayton felt as if he were in a dream as he obeyed. He was sworn in, and then Frank Amos grasped his hand and shook it.

'You've got a big score to settle against these bad men, Troy,' he said. 'And you've got the backing of the most powerful men in Bender County. But what you have to do must be done alone. Those crooks won't give in without a fight. Do you think you can handle it?'

'As I see it, I have to clean out Kline and his men, and keep Pete Bolam alive. After that I'll take on anyone who wants to argue with me. But what happens if Kline and his deputies put up a fight and I have to kill any of them?'

'While you're wearing that badge and following the dictates of the oath you swore then you can do no wrong,' Wade said. 'It's your play now, Troy.'

'As the town marshal do I have an office somewhere around here?' Clayton asked.

Wade nodded, his expression grim. 'It's in the county sheriff's office. Do you think you can handle that?'

'I'll handle it.' Clayton nodded. He turned to the door and departed, determined to make a start on the chore he had come back to do. In the back of his mind was the thought that perhaps he was being used by the leading men of the county for their own purposes. But he contented himself with the knowledge that if their desires coincided with his own then he could not go wrong.

9

In the darkness of the street, Clayton paused and looked around, gripped by powerful emotions. The frustrations and injustices of the past seven years were bottled up inside him, and a tumultuous surge of hatred against the unknown men responsible for them overwhelmed him. A cold sweat broke out on his forehead. He drew his gun, checked the loads, and slid it back into its holster, easing it so that it rode easy on his hip. He was as ready as he would ever be to start collecting the grim debts owed to him.

So his years of running and hiding were over. He felt lightheaded at the thought. And the men responsible for his plight were still walking around this town as if they owned it. He pictured Kline's beefy face, and fought down an urge to hasten to the law office and shoot the overweight sheriff full of holes. He glanced down at the law star pinned to his shirt, touched the cold, shiny metal which gave him authority, and wondered at the turn-around in his fortunes.

He started along the sidewalk, his heels rapping smartly on the boards. Walking to the sheriff's office, he paused to peer in through the front window, and smiled when he saw Kline seated at his desk.

Pushing open the door, Clayton entered the office and closed the door with his heel, eyes fixed upon the obese sheriff with all the intensity of a snake watching its prey. Kline looked up, and then froze. His fleshy face became stiff with fear. His eyes quickly filled with the terror of one who is instinctively aware that he has reached the end of his trail.

The glinting marshal's badge on Clayton's shirt mesmerized Kline. He stared at it in disbelief. His mouth gaped and breath hissed between his thick lips.

Clayton felt a cold rage mounting inside him. His right hand was down at his side, and he could feel the butt of his deadly gun against the inside of his wrist.

'On your feet, Kline,' he rapped.

The sheriff pushed himself upright, overturning his chair in his haste. He lifted his hands shoulder high without being told. Fear was a pale stain on his beefy features. Clayton looked at him and was filled with revulsion.

'You low skunk!' His voice shook with rage. 'You ran me out of the county and lied about what I was supposed to have done. You and Pete Bolam. Well the boot is on the other foot now. Take a good look at the badge they pinned on me. It gives me all the rights I need to settle your hash, and those you schemed with.'

'They made you the town marshal?' Kline shook his head. 'Do they figure you're good enough to smash the set-up

205

around here? I sure would like to see you go up against Brady's hired guns. You don't have a prayer, Clayton.'

'You won't be around to see it.' Clayton looked around the office, seeing it as it was seven years before, when Kline had first put him behind bars. The big cage at the rear of the office was gone now, and there was a door in the back wall that gave access to the new cell block built at the rear. 'Get rid of your gun-belt, Kline.'

The sheriff obeyed cautiously, moving slowly, his gaze fixed upon Clayton's taut face. He stepped sideways away from his fallen hardware. Clayton smiled.

'Let's take a look at your cells, huh?'

Kline motioned to the desk, and Clayton saw a bunch of keys lying on a corner. He nodded.

'Get moving. I want this town cleaned up by midnight.'

Kline grabbed the keys and unlocked the door in the back wall. He led the way into the cell block, and Clayton, following closely, found himself in a passage which ran the whole length of the building. There were three doors on the left, the first of which was marked TOWN MARSHAL. Beyond the doors was a large cell with a barred front, and on the right were four single cells.

Clayton holstered his gun, spun the sheriff around and quickly ran his hands over the man's rock-like figure. He discovered a .41 hideout gun in a holster in Kline's left armpit and stuck it into the back of his belt.

'Any cell you fancy being locked up in?' he demanded. 'You can take your pick. It looks like you don't have any customers in here. But all that is gonna change now. This place will be filled to overflowing by the time I get through.'

Kline made no reply and Clayton pushed him into the nearest cell and locked the door. The sheriff turned and looked at him.

'You got anything to say before I start cleaning up?'

Kline shook his head and dropped

heavily on to the foot of the bed in the cell. Clayton drew a long, ragged breath and went back to the office. He locked the connecting door, and, as he turned to survey the office, the street door was thrust open and five men entered, led by Slick Porter, who stepped aside to close the door as the others crowded in off the street. Clayton saw that Barney and Bolam were two of the newcomers, and they were being handled roughly by the others.

'We found 'em like you said, Sheriff,' Porter announced, slamming the door. 'They was snug in bed at the doc's.'

The two men holding Barney and Bolam halted when they saw Clayton. Barney's eyes widened when he spotted the law badge on Clayton's shirt front. Porter turned from the door, and halted as if he had run into a wall. Then he made a play for his holstered gun. Clayton waited until Porter had almost cleared leather, then responded by drawing his own weapon. The deadly sixgun was cocked and levelled before

Porter could begin to lift his Colt.

Porter stayed his movement and his hand fell away from his holster. His eyes betrayed great shock.

'Barney, can you get their guns?' Clayton asked. 'They look like they don't want a fight.'

'Can I!' Barney, his face still pale from the shock of his wound, immediately rounded on the men and disarmed them. He took Porter's gun and thrust the man forward to join the other two.

Clayton unlocked the connecting door and they ushered the prisoners into the cell block and locked them in the big cell.

'Not you, Pete,' Clayton said, and Bolam halted. He was unsteady on his feet, and Barney supported him. Clayton opened the door of the town marshal's office and looked inside. There was a small window overlooking the back lots, which was heavily barred, and a cot in a corner. 'In here, Pete. You get special treatment.'

'If you think I'm gonna talk then you

better think again,' Bolam rapped.

'I don't need you to talk now. My problems have been sorted out. But I don't want Brady getting to you so I'm keeping you safe inside, and if you've got any sense you'll stay quiet.'

He went around the office looking for weapons, found none, and locked Bolam inside. Going back into the front office, he motioned for Barney to sit down, and the old man sighed with relief as he did so.

'I don't know what's happened since you left the doc's, Troy, but it's obvious that something's gone right for you. I got the shock of my life when I saw you in here with that law star pinned to your shirt. And you've already thrown Kline and Porter into a cell.'

'I'll tell you about it later, Barney. What I need to know right now are the men I can expect trouble from. If I can round them up before word gets out that I've taken over then Brady won't be able to resist.'

'There's only Kline and Porter with

law stars. The rest of the men Kline uses are hard cases who hang around town. But it will be a different matter with Brady. He keeps a few gunhands around at all times. Usually they're in Brady's saloon along the street, and ready to do Brady's dirty work at the drop of a hat.'

'How are you feeling? Are you up to keeping my prisoners behind bars?'

'I can do that,' Barney nodded. 'But you'll need me to go with you around town. I can point out the hard cases who should be behind bars.'

Clayton shook his head. 'I don't want you getting mixed up in this any more than you have to. I'll play it as it comes. Lock the door here, and keep it locked until I return. Don't answer to anyone. I'll sing out when I come back.'

Barney nodded doubtfully. Clayton left the office and strode along the sidewalk. When he reached dense shadow he stepped into it and paused to look around. There appeared to be three saloons along the street, and all seemed to be busy. He was standing almost opposite the hotel, and on impulse he went across the street and peered into the hotel lobby.

Madge Austin was sitting behind the reception desk, and, when Clayton saw that the lobby was otherwise deserted, he entered and confronted the woman.

'Howdy?' he said, and she gazed at Troy for a moment before recognizing him. Her changing expression alerted him, for she was immediately on the defensive.

'You shouldn't be wandering around the town openly,' she said quickly. 'Every man is watching for you.'

'That's nothing new,' he responded. 'Can you tell me where Hudson Brady lives?'

'He has rooms over the top of his office, just along the street to the left. You can't miss it. His name is plastered all over the front of the building.' She spotted the marshal's badge and surprise stained her face. 'Where did you get that badge from? There hasn't been a marshal in Sunset Ridge for years. Kline won't have a marshal around.'

'He didn't object when I saw him earlier.' Clayton smiled. 'Thanks for the information.'

He turned on his heel and departed, walking to the left until he reached a brick two-storey building that had a large sign out front bearing Hudson Brady's name. The ground floor was in darkness, but there were lighted windows on the first floor, and he saw a flight of wooden steps at the side of the building.

Ascending the steps, he tried the door at the top and found it locked. Rapping heavily, he waited patiently for a reply, and when the door was jerked open by a tough-looking man he smiled.

'Who are you and what do you want?' the man demanded. He was wearing twin sixguns on crossed cartridge-belts around his waist The holsters containing the guns were tied down with leather thongs around the thighs. A quick-draw gunnie guarding Hudson. Clayton steadied his breathing.

'I'm the new town marshal and I need to see Brady,' he replied.

The man frowned. He looked at the law badge as if he had never seen one before.

'Is Brady in?' Clayton demanded.

'Sure he is, but he ain't seeing anyone this time of day.'

'He'll see me.' Clayton stepped forward as if to enter and triggered an immediate response from the gunnie. The man raised a hand to Clayton's right shoulder to prevent him entering, and Clayton grasped the wrist, twisted it sharply, and used his considerable strength to thrust the man back across the threshold.

The man sprawled on his face and rolled across the floor then came to his feet, both hands flashing to his holstered guns. Clayton reached for his gun and cleared leather. The big weapon blasted out a single shot and the gunman took the bullet in the centre of his chest. He went over backwards, arms flying wide, and crashed on to the floor on his back. Blood quickly spread on the pale blue fabric of his shirt.

A door opened and Hudson Brady looked out of an inner room. Clayton cocked his gun and pointed the muzzle at the big man. Brady stared at him, then came fully into the room. He looked at the badge on Clayton's chest, then glanced down at his man on the floor.

'What's going on?' he demanded.

'I came to talk to you,' Clayton replied. 'I'd like to know why, after seeing me on Double B range this morning, you went to the ranch and sent four gunnies out after me. I had to shoot two of them, and Barney Draper was wounded.'

'I didn't send anyone out after you.' Brady shook his head. 'Those men were a regular patrol watching for rustlers, and they made the mistake of tangling with you. Did you have to kill Toomey?'

'He drew on me. I didn't have a choice.'

'How come you're wearing the marshal's badge? Who offered you the job?'

'I'm taking you to the jail.' Clayton waggled his gun. 'If you're armed then get rid of it now, and do it slow. Are you alone up here?'

'There's no one else. I'm not armed.'

'Come on then. I don't have to warn you about trying to resist, do I?'

'Why would I resist?' Brady shook his head. 'I haven't broken the law. Where is Kline? Does he know about this?'

'He's in the office, and he doesn't know about this.'

'Then I'll talk to him.' Hudson came forward and Clayton allowed him to pass. He followed the big man out of the building and they crossed the street and walked silently to the jail. They had barely reached the opposite sidewalk when a harsh voice called to Clayton from behind.

'Hold it right there. Boss, where are you going? What was that shot fired in your apartment?'

Clayton turned slowly to see two gunmen coming across the street from Hudson's place. Both men were holding guns, and Clayton started shooting without warning. His first shot took the nearest man through the centre of the chest, and he fired a second shot before the other man could get his gun working. The crash of the shooting sent echoes across the silent town, and Clayton turned back to Hudson before the two gunmen had finished falling to the ground.

'You've sure got yourself well protected,' Clayton observed. 'Are there many more of these two-bit gunnies around?'

'More than you can handle,' Hudson replied. 'They all have instructions to watch out for me. But it looks like I'm employing the wrong kind of men. You should be on my payroll. What about it? Are you interested in an easy job with plenty of money? You could boss my gun crew.'

'No.' Clayton spoke grimly. 'Let's get on to the jail before any more of your guns show up.'

They reached the law office and Clayton sang out to warn Barney, who opened the door, a gun in his hand.

'I was getting worried,' Barney said. 'I heard the shooting and imagined all sorts of bad things. But here you are with Hudson Brady hisself. Well if that don't beat all.'

'Brady wants to talk to Kline,' Clayton replied.

'Sure.' Barney grinned. 'That can be arranged. Come on in, Brady. Kline's got plenty of time to listen to you.'

Clayton watched Brady intently as they took the man into the cell block, and Brady pulled up in mid-stride when he saw Kline behind bars. He turned on Clayton, his heavy eyelids partially obscuring his pale eyes. He blinked rapidly, and Clayton saw respect showing in his gaze before

Brady wiped all expression from his features.

'Looks like you won the first hand,' he observed, 'but the game ain't over yet, not by a long rope. If you're still around town when word of this gets out then you'll be down in the dust before the sun comes up.'

Clayton made no reply. Barney unlocked a cell door and motioned for Brady to enter. The big man looked as if he would refuse, then nodded and entered the cell. Barney closed the door with a metallic crash and jangled his bunch of keys after he had locked it. He led the way back to the office.

'I've killed three men getting Brady here,' Clayton said bitterly. 'I was hoping to do this without bloodshed.'

'I don't think that is possible.' Barney shook his head. 'Like Brady says, we'll be knee-deep in his gunnies when word gets out that you've arrested him. And what do you figure will happen when Chuck Brady out at Double B learns that his father has been throwed in jail?'

Clayton nodded. 'I know it won't be any picnic, but I'm playing it as it comes.'

A fist hammered on the street door and Clayton palmed his gun as he crossed to it. When he opened it he saw Doc Amos and the mayor standing there, with almost a dozen men at their backs.

'We've been busy too, and got some help for you,' the mayor said with a grin. 'We figured we couldn't throw you in at the deep end and just leave it to you. These men are law abiding. Swear them in as special deputies and they'll back you all the way.'

'There are dead gunmen out on the street,' Doc Amos observed. 'Brady's men. Have you seen Hudson Brady?'

'We sure have,' Barney cut in. 'I locked him in a cell out back. You wanta take a look at him?'

'I need to rid the town of Brady's men,' Clayton said.

'You need to handle the important points,' the mayor pointed out. 'Leave these men to round up the hard cases.'

Bill Coppard came into the office. The lawyer was carrying a slim black leather case under one arm.

'I'd like to get a statement from Kline,' he said crisply. 'As County Prosecutor I need to start building a case against the men you've arrested.'

Clayton nodded, out of his depth with such matters. But he saw how quickly order was established in the office. Groups of new deputies went out to patrol the town, and soon began to return with known trouble-makers in custody. Three men were ensconced in the office to hold it against any attempts at breaking out the prisoners.

At midnight, Clayton made a round of the town and was satisfied with what he found. The saloons were closed and no one moved around the main street. But he was not fooled by the peaceful atmosphere. No doubt riders had already ridden out for Double B, and if Chuck Brady brought in his outfit they would be knee-deep in gun trouble.

10

Clayton was fascinated by the way Bill
Coppard went about his job of
collecting evidence from the prisoners.
The lawyer had Sheriff Kline brought
out of the cells to be interrogated, and
Clayton remained in the background,
listening and watching. At first, Kline
was arrogant and refused to answer any
questions. But Coppard's quietly insis-
tent voice began to wear him down.
Kline's manner changed and he began
to answer defensively, giving away
nothing of his guilt, until he had to start
putting forward names of men who
could be guilty in his place. Then he
became apprehensive, and, when he
began to contradict himself, Coppard
struck with the speed of a snake.

But the sheriff was a hard man to
break, and Coppard had him returned
to his cell before the interrogation was

finished. The lawyer smiled at Clayton as Kline was led away.

'Don't look so tense, Troy,' he said. 'I've made good progress with Kline. Another session like that and he'll be singing hymns if I ask him. Now I'd like to lock horns with Pete Bolam. I've got here the statement he made at your trial seven years ago, in which he says he witnessed you committing the robbery. I can see some interesting points in it that need further explanation, and Bolam will hang himself if I give him enough rope for the job.'

Clayton shook his head. 'I can't watch this,' he said, 'it's too nerve-racking. I'll take a look around town.'

He left the office as Bolam was brought out to face the lawyer, and saw fear in the man's eyes as Bolam sat down across the desk from Coppard. He closed the street door on the scene and drew a deep breath of the cold night air. When he looked around he was surprised to see grey streaks raking the sky. The night had passed away and a new day was breaking.

He sighed deeply, slightly shocked by the astonishing turn of events that had overtaken him. The door opened at his back and Doc Amos emerged from the office.

'It's been a long night,' Amos said, breathing deeply.

'I just surprised myself by noticing dawn coming in,' Clayton responded. 'I didn't know time could go so fast.'

'The last seven years must seem like a lifetime to you.' Amos placed a hand on Clayton's shoulder. 'But it is working out well, Troy. You've taken it in your stride, and it's nearly done now. Coppard is convinced he'll have all the statements he'll need to make charges stick against Kline and Brady that will put them away for a long time. He's working on Bolam now, and Pete is gonna come out on your side when he sees which way the wind is blowing.'

'I can't see that happening.' Clayton shook his head.

Amos laughed. 'Don't worry about it.

Coppard will get at the truth now that Kline is no longer handling the investigation. The truth will come out.'

Clayton shrugged. 'I'll take a walk around town. My head is spinning with all the doubts and suspicions I got in my mind. I have to be ready for Chuck Brady if he rides in with his outfit. There could be a lot of trouble around town when the sun comes up.'

'Nothing will happen that you can't handle,' Amos told him. 'But watch your back, Troy.'

Clayton nodded and went along the sidewalk, walking slowly, checking his surroundings every step of the way. The tip of the sun was beginning to show above the eastern horizon in a fury of scarlet and crimson that clawed and streaked the heavens. Shadows were dissipating, fleeing imperceptibly. Range of vision increased, and the bare bones of the town lay exposed to Clayton's analytical gaze.

It had been too long since he had looked upon this street with freedom in his heart. He could remember being thrust into the stagecoach that had taken him to prison, with irons on his limbs and a grinning Hondo Kline herding him with a sawn-off shotgun in hand. It was a nightmare that had never deserted him. But now it seemed to fade into insignificance as he touched the glinting law star pinned to his shirt front. He was not certain how the change had come about, but it was for real.

He walked the length of the main street before retracing his steps to the law office. He was halfway back, opposite the bank, when the sudden thud of approaching hoofs alerted him. He paused and turned in the direction of the sound, and his lips pulled tight against his teeth when he saw seven riders cantering through the thick dust of the wide street, a closely knit bunch motivated by one thought and working together as one man.

He was spotted immediately, and the foremost of the riders jerked on his reins and brought his horse to a halt at the edge of the sidewalk where Clayton was standing. The other six riders grouped together behind him, hard-eyed men who were clearly not ordinary ranch-hands. Without exception the six men sat their mounts with right hands resting lightly on their right thighs, conveniently close to their holstered guns.

'What have we got here?' The foremost rider was young, in his early twenties. He was dressed in expensive range clothes that showed no signs of toil. His eyes were shadowed by the wide brim of his black Stetson. 'Who are you?'

Clayton recognized Chuck Brady. Seven years ago Chuck had been a mere youth. The intervening years had filled him out and coarsened him, and he was the image of Hudson, his father.

'I know who you are,' Clayton countered.

'Troy Clayton.' One of the gunnies spoke softly. 'I saw you three years ago at Indian Creek. You killed three men who were gun-sharping for Joseph Hain. The way I saw it, they didn't have a prayer. They started the play but you stiffened all three before they could get their guns working. I never saw gunplay like that before or since. I don't want any part of this, Chuck. If you're gonna bust your pa outa jail then you'll do it without me while Troy Clayton is standing against you.'

'You got some almighty good sense,' Clayton observed. 'I'm standing for the law, and I put your pa behind bars during the night, Chuck. If he's innocent he'll be turned loose. But while I'm wearing this badge no one, but no one, is gonna come into town and talk about busting prisoners out of the jail.'

Chuck Brady's fleshy face turned pale as blood ebbed from his features. There was rabid defiance in his eyes, and Clayton could sense that the youngster was going to ignore his grim warning.

'I don't take that kind of talk from no one,' Brady snapped. 'More especially from a thief and killer who slunk away from here seven years ago with his tail between his legs.'

Clayton was watching the men grouped beyond Brady. Tall, lean men of action, bronzed by many years of riding the back trails of the country, all had the same look of cold efficiency about them as they returned his stare impersonally. The gunman who had recognized Clayton was sitting on the left of the group, and, as Clayton watched, he wheeled his mount aside and rode off to the left.

'I don't want no part of this,' he said loudly as he moved. 'I'm about to make tracks for other parts. I quit, Chuck.'

'Yeller belly!' Brady snarled, and set his hand into frenzied motion, reaching for the flared butt of the big sixgun in the holster on his hip.

Clayton's lean-muscled body did not move. His cold, unwavering gaze was holding all these men within its compass, and he was hair-triggered to react to the first hostile movement from any one of them. Brady's movement took them all along with him, including Clayton, and he was faster by far.

Red flame licked out from the long-barrelled sixshooter that appeared as if by magic in Clayton's hand. Chuck Brady did not finish his draw. His gunhand faltered as a half-inch chunk of lead blasted into his breastbone. He fell backwards and sprawled sideways out of his saddle, spoiling the action of the two men on his left. Gun thunder bludgeoned the silence, sending echoes chasing across the silent town as Clayton fired his gun rapidly until the hammer finally dropped on an empty shell.

The three gunmen who were clear of Brady to the right managed to get their guns into their hands, but two of them were dead before they could fire. The third tried desperately to level up on Clayton, and died with a bullet in his throat as Clayton's deadly gun fired inexorably.

The two gunmen who had become entangled with the dying Brady cursed and tried to get their weapons working. By then the shooting was at an end, and they found themselves sitting their horses alone, staring into the smoking muzzle of Clayton's gun. Clayton's face was hard and unemotional.

'Drop your guns or work them,' he rasped.

The men obeyed instantly. Both opened their fingers and their guns fell to the street. They raised their hands, and the gunman who had pulled out before the shooting started sat his mount on the sideline and shook his head wordlessly at what he had seen.

'Pick up Brady and take him along to the livery barn,' Clayton ordered. 'You men can stay there until I come for you or you can ride out. If you do leave town then don't ever come back. Now move.'

He watched them follow his instructions, and caught a movement off to his left as he reloaded the spent chambers of his gun. He tensed, thumbing back his hammer, then saw Barney Draper waiting with a shotgun in his hands. The old man was shaking his head, his wrinkled face showing disbelief.

Clayton eased forward his hammer, but before he could holster his gun he heard the sound of rapidly approaching hoofs and the grating of wheels coming from the other direction along the street. Turning swiftly, his eyes narrowed against the growing sunlight, he hefted his gun, ready for action. A buggy, apparently being chased at a distance by two riders, was coming into town fast, with dust broiling up from its wheels. Barney came forward to Clayton's side.

'That's Helen on the buggy,' he said. 'With Hoke McGee chasing her.' Clayton stepped into the street and moved out to its centre, facing the oncoming buggy, and Helen immediately swerved towards him. Her face was pale, strained, showing extreme fear, and, as she whipped the horse unmercifully, her voice slashed through the silence.

'McGee is trying to kill us!'

The two riders were fifty yards behind the buggy but gaining fast, and they immediately reined in at the sound of the girl's voice. Clayton saw McGee lift a sixgun to take aim at Helen. He fired instantly, shooting past the buggy. His bullet took McGee in the chest and the big man dropped his gun, flung his arms wide, then pitched backwards out of his saddle to flop into the dust of the street. The second rider immediately swung his horse and rode into an alley.

Clayton grabbed the reins of the horse pulling the buggy as it careered past him and brought it to a halt. Dust flew. He peered at the girl on the seat and saw, with growing shock, that the other figure hunched beside her was his father. Henry Clayton was conscious, his ashen face showing the ravages of the wound he had received, but he was aware of his surroundings, and gazed at Troy with an unblinking stare.

'Troy!' Helen's expression was filled with disbelief as she stared at him. 'You! That badge! What's going on?'

'You tell me.' His eyes were upon his father. Henry Clayton looked to be on the point of collapse.

Barney came up, his face set in grim lines. 'More riders coming in,' he said, jerking a thumb into the direction from which the buggy had come.

Clayton swung around and saw ten riders some two hundred yards distant, coming at a fast clip along the street.

'More Tented C riders,' he observed. 'What's going on? Why was McGee out to kill you, Helen?'

'Ask Howard.' Henry Clayton spoke in a wavering voice. 'He shot me in the back in Water Gully. Pete Bolam sent me a message, saying he was leaving the country and if I paid him a thousand dollars he'd give me some information

I'd be glad to hear. I saw Bolam and he told me the truth about you, Troy. Bolam lied about seeing you doing the robbery. And it was Howard who paid him to lie. Howard confronted me in Water Valley when I was on my way back to the ranch after seeing Bolam, and when I challenged him about Bolam's accusation he drew his gun and shot me in cold blood.'

'Howard!' Troy Clayton lifted his gaze to the approaching riders. He could see his brother was leading them, holding a sixgun, urging the riders with him to greater effort. He shook his head. 'I can't get my mind around this,' he said. 'Howard! But he's my brother, and I never did a thing against him.'

'You did one thing,' Henry said harshly. 'You were born my son. Howard was always jealous of you. It became a sickness with him. I was aware of it, and I guess I didn't think it was too serious. But I should have watched him more closely. I'm sorry, Troy, for failing you, Son.'

Clayton shook his head. 'Get the buggy out of here,' he rapped. 'Pull along the street, Helen. I'll stop Howard here.' He slapped the rump of the horse and the buggy swept away.

Barney cocked his shotgun. His face was resolute. When he glanced at Clayton and met his gaze his eyes were filled with determination. Clayton checked his gun.

'I always suspected there was something wrong with Howard,' Barney said through his teeth. 'I noticed many little things over the years. But I didn't think he was this bad.'

Clayton said nothing. He watched the oncoming riders. His thoughts were slow, sluggish, as if shock was preventing the grim truth from getting through to him. Howard had always picked on him, had never done a thing for him, and now, it seemed, he had been the originator of all the grim events that had occurred from the moment of that false accusation seven years ago.

'Barney, you better get to cover,'

Clayton said suddenly. 'It looks like there'll be shooting, and it ain't your fight.'

'Ain't it hell?' Barney waggled the shotgun. 'It's been your fight alone far too long. But you ain't alone any more. Take a look around you.'

Clayton shifted his gaze, and was surprised to see Doc Amos standing by the buggy, which had halted outside the law office. He was in the process of helping Henry Clayton out of the vehicle. On the nearby sidewalk most of the special deputies were grouped together, all pointing weapons at the oncoming riders. Clayton shook his head. He didn't want wholesale slaughter. This was still his fight. His and Howard's. Howard had been pushing for this from the day Troy Clayton had been born.

'Hold up there, you riders,' he called, and his voice echoed around the street. 'Turn around and leave town. Howard, you keep on coming. There's something we got to settle.'

'It's all settled now,' Howard yelled, and spurred his horse forward, raising dust as he rode straight for his motionless brother. He was waving his sixgun in the air but not pointing it at anyone in particular.

Troy stood motionless with his gun down at his side. He watched Howard carefully, wondering if he could bring himself to shoot his brother if Howard tried to kill him. His mind was seething with the knowledge that Howard had framed him with the robbery and then dry-gulched their father.

Barney lifted his shotgun into the aim, settling the butt into his shoulder. He squinted along the twin barrels at the advancing rider.

'If you don't shoot him, I will, Troy,' he warned.

Howard was twenty yards away and rapidly drawing closer. Troy stood as if turned to stone. Barney eared back the hammers on the shotgun. Then Howard levelled his pistol, aiming at Troy, who braced himself but did not attempt to defend himself. Howard fired, gun-smoke blossoming around his head and shoulders. Troy heard the crackle of the bullet passing his left ear.

Barney yelled a warning to Howard, who ignored it. He lifted his gun for a second shot, and at that moment a rifle cracked from some place behind Troy. A bullet took Howard in the forehead and he crumpled instantly. His gun flew from his hand and he pitched sideways, slumping out of the saddle as the horse ran on. He hit the ground hard and lay inert.

Clayton drew a shuddering breath as the echoes of the shots faded away. A keen breeze was blowing into his face but the smell of gunsmoke suddenly sickened him. He blinked, and slowly became animated. He braced his shoulders and turned to look around, and a pang stabbed through him when he saw his father standing with a rifle to his shoulder still sighting the weapon at the spot where he had sent a killing shot into his eldest son in order to save the life of his youngest.

Barney lowered his shotgun. 'Damn it all!' he cursed. 'But it's done, Troy.'

'Yeah.' Troy nodded. 'Looks like it's all over at last.'

'All bar the shouting!' Barney looked around. 'And there's gonna be a lot of that, Troy. Welcome home, Son.'

Clayton looked at the body of Howard lying crumpled in the dust, and turned his head to see Helen running towards him from the buggy. He had come home to avenge the death of his father, or so he had thought. But Fate had decreed otherwise. His father had survived against all the odds, and Troy Clayton was reinstated in the county.

Justice had been served. The knowledge filtered through him as he holstered his gun. The bitterness in his heart was slowly turning to dust. He looked at Helen's eager face as she came to him, remembering what they had felt for each other seven long years ago. He instinctively held out a hand to her. She grasped it, and together they turned to go to his father, who was waiting grimly to welcome him, but not as the returning prodigal.

THE END